The Bartender's Guide To Murder

DEATH AS A FINE ART

ALSO BY
SHARON LINNÉA

FICTION

Death in Tranquility (Bartender's Guide to Murder 1)

Death By Gravity (Bartender's Guide to Murder 2)

Death Among the Stars (Bartender's Guide to Murder 3)

Death from Beyond (Bartender's Guide to Murder 4)

WITH B.K. SHERER

Chasing Eden

Beyond Eden

Treasure of Eden

Plagues of Eden

YOUNG ADULT, WITH AXEL AVIAN

Colt Shore: Domino 29

NONFICTION

Princess Ka'iulani: Hope of a Nation, Heart of a People

Raoul Wallenberg: The Man Who Stopped Death

Chicken Soup from the Soul of Hawai'i

Lost Civilizations

America's Famous and Historic Trees with Jeff Meyer

DEATH AS A FINE ART

SHARON LINNÉA

COCKTAIL RECIPES BY JAMIELYNN BRYDALSKI

Arundel
PUBLISHING

The Bartender's Guide to Murder Book 5

Death as a Fine Art

Copyright @ 2024

Lyrics from "My Mother's Savage Daughter" © 1990 Karen L. Unrein (Kahan). All rights reserved.

ISBN 978-1-933-608-47-1 (paperback)

ISBN 978-1-933-608-45-7 (digital online)

First edition December 2024

Cover Art and Cover Design by David Colón

Interior Design by Phillip Gessert

For all the Savage Daughters

1
I THINK WE HAVE A SITUATION

T HE GINGERBREAD MAN was dead in the lobby.

This was the ultimate surprise in an afternoon of unexpected events. I honestly thought we'd already awarded shock of the year, but by anyone's account, the demise of Noel Schlessinger topped them all.

Here's how it went down.

It was a crisp Friday afternoon in mid-November and I was in the Battened Hatch, the Scottish pub attached to the inn misleadingly named MacTavish's Seaside Cottages. Misleading because there is no sea and there are no cottages. There is, however, a MacTavish, scion of the family who'd run the inn for over one hundred years. The inn itself is magnificent and woodsy and one-of-a-kind. It pours out of the hockey-rink-sized lobby in three directions, hallways meandering the hills of Tranquility, New York, an Adirondack town that had twice hosted the Winter Olympics.

Though the cavernous lobby is made of dark wood, light floods it both from skylights and a back wall of floor-to-ceiling windows, which provide a panoramic view of a small lake encircled by old-growth forest. A huge statue of downhill skiers, seemingly whooshing from one of the skylights, bestows upon the lobby a feeling of movement and excitement. Near the statue stands a maroon circular sofa, known in bygone days as a banquette settee. Its center pillar anchored a ring of seats facing outward, perilously close to the skiers' path— giving the impression that unwary loungers could easily be whacked by the skiers.

We'll get back to that settee.

On the far side of the lobby are two doors. One is chrome and glass, usually set wide open, welcoming all comers. It leads into a restaurant named Pepper's, a pricy, upscale place that overlooks the lake and caters to the tourist trade.

To the right of this entrance is an undistinguished wooden door. The small, painted pub sign above it features a masted sailing ship cutting through waves above the words That Ship Has Sailed.

Through that door is a dark hallway that smells of wood polish and leather. It is the only working time machine I know of. At least, it functions as one for me, leading back into a past that doesn't normally exist; a past in which mahogany bars were lined with larger-than-life characters sipping extraordinary concoctions, alcoholic or not, created by the local barkeep and mixologist.

In this case, that would be me.

Those in the know call the pub by its local nickname, The Battened Hatch.

That's where I stood that autumn afternoon, along with Marta Layton, my assistant manager and bartender-in-training. While teal-colored hair came and went from everyone else's fashion statements, Marta's highlights stayed firm.

In front of the bar sat a blonde woman.

She had said hello, calling me by name. Without thinking, I had answered in kind as she slipped onto a comfortable, cushioned bar chair. As she sat, so did a large gentleman—in his early sixties was my best guess. He had a face with animated features highlighted by male pattern baldness, and the squarest forehead I'd ever seen. He wore a tan jacket. "Hey," he said, in a way that implied he had now arrived and any other patrons or conversations could wait. "Hey. Gimme a hot chocolate and bourbon."

As he spoke, the door from the kitchen swung open behind me and Stormie Edwards, Chef Angelica Dormer's sous chef, bounced through. "Avalon!" she said, "Have you heard who's here—"

Stormie's eyes landed on the woman in front of me and she

screeched to a halt. "Um," she pivoted, "the first contestant has arrived. For the gingerbread house competition. It's real, and it's happening!"

As she turned back around, she gave a silent scream which could be seen only by Marta and myself. It was clearly referencing said woman.

"When does the competition begin?" I asked, partly to help bolster her flimsy cover story, partly to torture her by not allowing her to escape her proximity to the actor whose fame had her hobbled, partly to postpone my own interaction with said movie star.

"The contestants arrive today and tomorrow. Filming starts on Saturday night."

"Filming?"

"Well, technically 'digitally recording' for the network. Yes, it's not like the National Gingerbread Competition at the Grove Park Inn in North Carolina. There, anyone can enter and the gingerbread creations arrive already fully built. Ours only has half a dozen preselected competitors, and they have to put the structures together here. They also have to incorporate some gingerbread they've cooked here on site. It's all being filmed—recorded--for the Delicious Network."

"They have to cook here? Where?"

Stormie nodded back toward the door she'd just come through.

"Angelica's kitchen?" I asked. "Strangers cooking in Chef Angelica's kitchen?"

"That's why it's a good thing she's away at the Brewster Competition, isn't it?"

"Chef doesn't *know*?"

"The local health inspector has signed off on it," she said quietly. "They'll use it in one-hour segments, overnight on Saturday. It will be pristine by Sunday morning."

As I continued to stare at her, she protested, "Mr. MacTavish is thrilled, you know that. Think of all the publicity it's bringing! And the hotel rooms will be full of contestants and television crew."

"This was your doing?" Truthfully, it was pretty impressive. And, as she said, Chef Angelica was away. I wondered sometimes if Sous Chef Stormie was a better fit at Pepper's than Chef Angelica. Did Stormie sometimes wonder that, too?

"That's why I'm here, Missy," said Mr. Hot-Chocolate-and-Bourbon. "I love to follow gingerbread competitions this time of year. They're so creative—and I love the drinks that come with them!"

I turned back around to the patron who had dared rename me Missy.

Okay, okay, yes. I was aware there was a Welcome to Gingerbread Land banner outside, and cards with the times of events and listings of gingerbread-themed drinks.

Which didn't mean I was ready for it to begin. I knew the contest had to be over before Thanksgiving so the houses could be on display starting Black Friday and running through the holiday season as a tourist draw.

That didn't mean I had hot chocolate at the ready. In my mind, that came after Thanksgiving, as we entered the Christmas/ski season. They weren't really planning to get this competition edited and running before Christmas, were they?

"You follow gingerbread competitions?" I asked my patron.

"Yes, indeed. I'm proudly known as the Gingerbread Man in some circles."

"How are you known in other circles?" I asked.

"Noel. Noel Schlessinger." I could detect a Long Island childhood in his accent. He reached out a beefy hand and gave mine a strong shake.

As we'd been discussing the cooking competition, staff and guests from around the hotel had been peeking in to get a gander at our famous guest, quietly seated next to Mr. Gingerbread. Some of them nonchalantly found tables, others just piled into each other, Keystone Cop style, at the end of the entry hall.

"Can you go into the kitchen and see what the hot chocolate situation is?" I asked Marta.

"Mom?" she whispered, referencing my earlier address of the celebrity seated before us. "You said, 'Hi, *Mom?*'"

I hoped she hadn't heard, or noticed, my shocked greeting. I'd hoped—and continued acting as if—no one did. Apparently, I was not so lucky.

I turned her around and shoved her through the swinging kitchen door.

"Coming right up," I said to Noel.

Then, with no further excuses for stalling, I turned to the A-list actor before me.

"Can I get you a drink?" I asked. "Or would you like to go somewhere and talk?"

"Sure," she said. "The second one."

"Back this way," I said.

She stood and Noel Schlessinger realized for the first time who he'd been seated next to. His jaw dropped. He sputtered, trying to talk, reaching out, but she was already beyond his grasp.

I led the way to the back wood-paneled hall. Did I mention I was wearing a cast? It was a walking cast and I told myself I was good at walking in it, but still, if you were trying to nonchalantly stride somewhere, it added its challenges.

I hobbled as quickly as I could.

Across from the restrooms was the bar's storeroom. No one had followed us—yet. Everyone in the bar was surely thinking of a reason they had to use the restroom. We had approximately ten seconds to disappear, by my reckoning.

I unlocked the storeroom door and we hurried inside, shutting and relocking it behind us. Not turning on the lights, I led us toward the back of the room, to keep our voices out of earshot. The storeroom is large, with two rows of shelving in the middle and heavier shelves against one wall. A refrigerated unit nestles across the other.

The room smelled faintly of fake lavender from a floor-cleaning product. There is no back window to allow in sunbeams and dust, only semi-darkness softened by the green letters of the exit sign and a light-sensitive nightlight I plugged in for occasions such as this.

In fact, I've had so many private conversations in the storeroom that in that moment, I decided to get a couple of chairs, a lamp, and a tufted rug. Beige, probably.

Dear God, I was thinking about anything in order to not to have to deal with the chiseled perfection in front of me.

"Avalon, what happened?" she nodded to the cast.

"Why are you here?" I asked.

"It's good to see you, too," said Anna Nash. "What happened?"

We looked at each other. I remembered almost dying once, and being sorry I hadn't made things right with her. I was so brimming with emotions—every single one ever invented—that their only escape route was a single tear, a warm streak down my cheek.

"I jumped off a building," I said. "It was on fire."

She pulled me to her. I didn't have the strength to fight her embrace. Even though I was in my late twenties, fitting into the space of my mother's arms, the familiar scent, the soft warmth of her sweater, the safety and danger promised there, I wept.

I am not an emotional person. I've been through a heck of a lot without losing my cool. Ask Mike Spaulding of the state police.

Mom always makes me lose my cool.

"Can you tell me what this is about?" she asked, referencing my outburst.

I shook my head. "Too much to go into."

She nodded. We moved to stand in the back corner by the night-light so we could see each other. She wore jeans and a beige sweater. Her natural blonde hair was a shade lighter than mine, brushing against her shoulders, molding her into a Nordic warrior. She worked out faithfully—she had to, it was part of the job. Her mus-cles were honed but not sharp. She wasn't tiny and elfin, she was statuesque, five eight, maybe? I'd never asked. But she gave off an aura which made her seem larger than life.

There is a ditty by Karen Kahan amongst the Nordic sisterhood which starts:

I am my mother's savage daughter,

The one who runs barefoot cursing sharp stones.

I am my mother's savage daughter,

I will not cut my hair, I will not lower my voice.

Those lyrics alone bring me strength in difficult situations. The thing is, there is nothing savage about my mother. She is kind. She is brilliant and brilliantly talented. She is funny, compassionate, willing to wade in to help in any given situation.

She is perfect.

Which makes it impossible to be furious with her, as, by definition, the problem has to be someone else's. Problems are for imperfect people.

Like me.

I wiped my cheeks with the back of my hands.

"I'm sorry we didn't get to spend more time together at your mormor's funeral," she said.

"Me, too."

"There's something I need to talk to you about, to do with changes in the family. Is there a time that would be good? After work, maybe?"

"I'm not closing tonight. I've promised to work a show at a local art gallery."

"After that? What time will you be done?"

"The show is seven to nine. I'll likely be done by nine-thirty. Is that too late? Will you still be here?"

"I'm here to talk to you," she said.

I knew what I should say next. I should offer her the guest room in my cottage. I should invite her into my life. The life I'd worked so hard to build here. The life where I was Avalon Nash, bartender and friend, not Avalon Nash, daughter of Anna Fucking Nash.

Not inviting her was quite obviously keeping her at arm's length. Worse, it amounted to throwing her to the public and the adoring fans.

"Do you have a place to stay?" I finally said.

"Yes. I have a room reservation here. I'm checking in under Anna Karenina," she smiled. She loved to borrow the monikers of famous Annas when she stayed in hotels. "But you have my number. We can text."

"I do," I said. "Will you be all right? People seem to have discovered you. Rise O'Connor was just here," I said, referencing a childhood friend who was now a well-known actor. "He had some challenges with people stalking him."

"Rise, really? How is the kid?"

"Complicated. I'll fill you in later."

"Okay. And don't worry. I can handle myself. When you act normal, people usually settle down."

Good luck with that, I thought.

"Text me when you're done," she said. "Quaint town. Think I'll look around."

"Okay. But Mom, be careful."

"I promise."

"Should I see if the coast is clear?" I asked, heading for the door.

"Naw. It's usually best to walk through and be gone before they realize you're there."

She put her hand on the doorknob. We nodded to each other. She opened it, stepped out—head high, smile on her face—and walked resolutely toward the exit door of the pub.

It worked. Everyone she passed stopped, as if turned to stone in her wake. And then she was gone.

Marta was at the bar, overseeing the influx of drink orders. I stepped back to help her.

"Mom?" she said again. "Hi, Mom?"

"Now you know," I said.

The next few hours flew by, as orders continued even though the unexpected guest had departed.

Things finally quieted down just before supper time, which was when Sous Chef Stormie reappeared from the kitchen behind me. She pulled me back away from the bar.

"I think we have a situation," she said.

"Oh?"

"Mr. Schlessinger, the guy who was sitting here, who called himself the Gingerbread Man? I saw him sitting in the lobby and I went to sit next to him to ask if he would enjoy being interviewed for the Delicious Network show."

"And?"

"He wouldn't answer me."

"Did he say maybe?"

"No, I mean, not at all. I think... I think he's dead."

I THINK WE HAVE A SITUATION

Ingredients

Cocktail (batch recipe)
3 quart saucepan
6 cups milk of your choice (preferably whole milk)
1 cup semi-sweet chocolate chips
1 tablespoon honey
1 vanilla bean
6 oz bourbon (your choice); set aside
Raw honeycomb or fresh honey for garnish
4 cocktail mugs

Whipped cream

1 large mixing bowl
3 cups heavy whipping cream
3 tablespoons honey
Remainder of vanilla bean seeds

Method

Hot Chocolate

Add milk to saucepan and stir until you have a gentle boil, continue stirring while adding the honey and semi-sweet chocolate chips. Slice vanilla bean down the center and scrape half of the seeds out and put into milk mixture in saucepan. Retain the rest for whipped crème. Continue to stir until all ingredients are mixed and then turn the heat down to low and let simmer for about 5 minutes stirring occasionally. Turn hot chocolate mixture off.

Whipped cream

Add all ingredients to large mixing bowl and whip (by hand or blender) until you have soft, fluffy peaks.

Cocktail

Add 1 1/2 oz of Bourbon to each cocktail mug, ladle hot chocolate mixture into each mug, leaving a space at the top for whipped cream. Add a few nice large dollops of whipped cream to top of hot chocolate bourbon mixture and finish with a small piece of fresh honeycomb or drizzle some fresh lose honey on top of crème.

2

THE AFOREMENTIONED SETTEE

"YOU THINK HE'S dead?"

Stormie nodded morosely. She was a medium-tall, young Black woman with hair so extravagant—long and dark brown with coil curls—I had no idea how she fit it all under a kitchen cap while she was working. Now that it was in between meal services, she let the curls fly, albeit held back with a colorful headscarf. She wore her chef's whites, of course.

I appreciated Stormie. She was down-to-earth, not easily rattled—how else could she have survived Chef Angelica thus far? And crazy talented. So I took her words seriously.

"Where?"

"In the lobby. On the round thing."

"The banquette settee?"

Another nod.

"Why are you telling me?"

"Who should I tell? Registration? Also, I'm not sure he's, you know."

Admittedly, I was known for having connections with local law enforcement. That didn't make *me* local law enforcement. I was still a normal citizen who didn't appreciate dealing with dead people.

If he was, indeed, dead.

I sighed, silently agreeing to scope out the situation. If I hobbled past and he was dead, I'd continue to security.

The lobby was alive with guests. A college hockey team was leaving, checking out after winning a big game at the arena next door.

Their whoops and hollers rose and fell. As a MacTavish employee, I was glad they'd stayed, not sorry they were heading out. Fortunately, none of them were paying attention to anything except their fellow victors.

Wearing a walking cast painted by a local artist and limping about in said cast is not the best way to deflect attention or fly under the radar. I put on my most nonchalant air and ventured toward the banquette, scanning the lobby for MacTavish's security folks. Nelson, the main man, was there, in his suit and badge, watching everything at once. He was tall—six two or so—hired to look intimidating, which he did. Naomi was behind the security desk. Neither seemed alarmed.

Mr. Schlessinger was seated there, alone, opposite the back windows. His eyes were open, his jacket closed. He looked normal.

Shoot.

I took a deep breath and went over, dropping onto the maroon cushioned seat next to the guest in question. "Mr. Schlessinger?" I asked. "Noel?"

He didn't respond. I finally brought myself to look over at him.

Wearing a cast, I tended to sit down hard. The simple act of my dropping next to him jostled him, opening his jacket an inch. Beneath it was a large circle of dark crimson. I could detect an odd, acrid smell in the air

No, no, no.

My breathing accelerated, as most anyone's would, sitting next to a corpse—although the tiniest part of me, even then, was grateful we hadn't somehow poisoned him with hot chocolate.

I knew the drill. First order of business, don't freak out the patrons. Well, not before the police and coroner arrived.

I did not want to be the one to call the authorities, not even the one alerting hotel security.

I wanted this not to have happened.

The gingerbread man had died from a gunshot wound to the chest. He'd been killed with a gun with a silencer, in a crowded lobby. Someone had done this on purpose. Someone who knew what they were doing. Someone who knew they'd be caught on camera.

Someone likely watching now.

I was tempted to scan the room. But if the killer was looking and we locked eyes, I'd have put a target over my own heart.

Instead, I stood as if nothing was amiss and limped back over through the door to Pepper's, where Stormie still stood, watching me.

I continued inside, toward the kitchen, out of sight of the lobby and motioned her back.

"You were right," I said to her. "He's dead. Gunshot to the chest."

As mentioned, Stormie was a trained chef, which means very little fazes her.

She was fazed.

"What do we do?"

"You know Nelson, the chief of security?"

"No."

"He's tall, wearing a suit and sunglasses and an earpiece. Hard to miss. You go to him and say you tried to talk to the guy on the settee but he seems unwell."

"So, send Nelson on a wellness check."

"That should take care of it."

"Now?" she was hesitant.

"We've got to get security on it before an unsuspecting hotel guest realizes there's a corpse in the lobby."

"You're sure it's not a heart attack?"

"Let's leave that to Nelson." Nope, wasn't a heart attack.

We walked together to the restaurant door, and she correctly identified the security man. I made a mental note to find out if Nelson was his first or last name, and what the other moniker was that went with it.

As Stormie headed across the lobby, I left Pepper's through the swinging door, walked through the kitchen which was gearing up for supper, and back into the Battened Hatch.

I took a deep breath.

"What's going on?" asked Marta.

"You still good to close tonight?" I asked.

"Yes."

"Good. Stay in here for the foreseeable future. We're not getting involved in whatever is going on in the lobby."

"Why? What's going on in the lobby?"

"Someone shot Noel Schlessinger."

Her eyes grew large. "Shot who?"

"The gingerbread man. Bourbon hot chocolate."

"No."

"Yes. And while you and I are used to helping the authorities solve this sort of stuff, I'm giving us the rest of the month off. We don't have to be part of any investigations till after Thanksgiving."

"What happens after Thanksgiving?"

"Nothing. Ever again. Hopefully."

"Okay. That would be good."

"Since I'm working the gallery opening tonight, I'm going to head out. You've got my number."

Marta nodded.

There is a sidewalk exit from the Battened Hatch. I never go out that way.

I went out that way.

There hadn't been a murder at this hotel since someone killed Joseph, the previous bartender at the Battened Hatch. His death left a job opening, which I'd filled. It had seemed only right—and prudent—to solve his murder under the circumstances.

But, on that November Friday, I was still pretending there could be a death investigation at MacTavish's which wouldn't involve me, and which certainly would not pose mortal danger to myself and those I love.

As if.

THE AFOREMENTIONED SETTEE

Ingredients

Sparkling wine
1 1/2 oz vodka
1 pound of fresh cherries (set some aside some for garnish)
1 cup of raw sugar
2 cups of water
Ice
Cocktail shaker
Medium saucepan
Fine mesh bar strainer
Nick and Nora glass

Method

Pit the cherries and cut into quarters. Add to water and sugar in sauce pan. Put on stove over medium heat, stirring ingredients until combined. Let simmer for about 20 minutes, stirring occasionally.
Remove cherries from heat and bring to room temperature. Strain cooled cherry combination through a colander making sure to save the liquid. Set aside and save the cherries for a charcuterie board.
In cocktail mixer, add vodka, 2 oz of cherry juice and ice. Shake and strain into the Nick and Nora glass. Top cocktail off with sparkling wine and fresh cherries.

3
GOLDEN LIGHT

Tranquility is a quaint town in upstate New York. The first thing anyone will tell you about is the Winter Olympics and that Tranquility played a pivotal role in making outdoor sports year-round in the United States, back in the day. Ice skating, snow skiing, hockey playing, luge, all became favorite hobbies here in the early 1900s.

Depending on which circles you run in, the second thing people might tell you about Tranquility is that it's the home of artist Michael Michel, known world-wide for his idealized paintings of the village's charming streets. He bathes our avenues and lanes in golden light, plunging the viewer into a psychological condition known as *hiraeth*. Hiraeth is a Welch word which describes a feeling of deep longing for a home that no longer exists—perhaps never did—but we know in our bones should exist. It's ours by right. If nothing else, we should be able to own a painting of it.

Thus, Michael Michel's paintings, prints, calendars, and note-cards sell for big bucks. Once a month, his gallery holds a reception for their patrons, possible patrons, and rich locals.

Twice a year, there is a gallery reception for the high rollers—if art sales used such a term. Invited are people who would pay beau-coup bucks for his huge, one-of-a-kind canvases—collectors, art dealers, gallery owners and the like. Tonight was one of those.

Was it surprising that I agreed to bartend this event?

Yes, indeed. For several good reasons.

Firstly, Mr. Michel's idealized representational works are not my cup of tea. Still, I would never hesitate to bartend at an event because I didn't like the artist's style.

My real issue is the painter, himself.

Michael Michel, aka The Painter Who Brings You Home©, is on the back side of middle-aged but looks like one would have imagined Michelangelo might have looked on a workday: large head, large nose, brownish-blonde shoulder-length hair, and a white artist's shirt that's always open a button too far. I'm sure he thinks himself to be windswept and sexy rather than on the prowl.

What else I know about him? He has a wife and seven children. My only glimpses of her involved herding her brood at the beginning of gallery shows. He's out and about quite often—though I've never seen him with a child—shopping, buying a pair of shoes, or sharing an ice cream cone.

As his occasional bartender, I know he favors Grey Goose vodka. Also, he knows without a doubt that when he graces a room, the rest of us mortals are damn lucky.

So why did I agree to bartend the event?

Easy. I'd worked one of his galas before and found it both entertaining and educational. They were attended by Tranquility's old guard, who spoke their unedited thoughts freely to each other—likely more candidly than they would in public spaces like MacTavish's. I loved watching people and learning how they think. It is one way a bartender's invisibility came in handy.

Main Street was chilly and dry, the one- and two-story shops still sporting autumnal pumpkins and horns of plenty. The local economy would much prefer the weather cold and wet. Winter sports depend on both snow and below freezing temperatures. Despite Thanksgiving's approach, the forecast showed no sign of precipitation. We did have an indoor hockey arena, but everything else was outdoors. Locals were getting nervous.

I was glad it wasn't raining, given my slower-than-usual pace. I'd disposed of my crutches the moment I'd left the hospital, but walking was slow and the cast rode up and down, chafing my skin.

The Welcome Home Gallery stood two doors past the movie theater. I paused briefly to steel myself before knocking. Usually, as "the help," I'd use the back entrance, but this was as far as I could make it.

Mona, the gallery manager, let me in and relocked the door behind me. She stared at my cast, undoubtedly wondering if I looked presentable enough. Beneath my coat, I wore bartender blacks, including wide-legged pants that mostly concealed the cast.

"I'll be behind the bar. No one will see it," I assured her.

"But can you stand up? Can you do the job?" she asked.

I promised I could. "Lainie, find a stool Avalon can sit on when she's not mixing drinks," she said.

No "how are you?" No "what happened?" No "wow, that's the most interestingly painted cast I've seen." Still, the offer of a stool was a kindness I hadn't expected.

"Thanks," I said.

"You've worked an opening before, you know the drill," she said, leading me to my station. No expense was spared at these events. The table was robed in a sky-blue linen cloth with smaller white cloths on top. Drink glasses (of real glass) were already set up. Red wine bottles stood like sentinels on the table, while whites chilled in a long, ice-filled planter. He was also serving good Champagne, but it was in silver ice buckets on the shelf behind me. You had to ask. Larger glasses for soft drinks were off to the side.

As before, a jar sat on the table, not for tips, but for contributions to the Drug Free Tranquility campaign. The irony of it sitting on a table dispensing liquor was not lost on me. I knew by now that contributions, made by check so the donor would be given full credit, would go towards the current mayor's next bid for office, three and a half years hence. Never too early to buddy up to him. Or to try to keep undesirables, such as nonrepresentational artists, out of our fair village.

Too late, Michael. Too late.

Even my cast was painted by a local nonrepresentational artist. I was very proud.

After checking the whole station, giving a quick glance to my hair and lipstick, I sat down on the cushioned stool. It was the first time I could take a breath.

The entire gallery was bathed in golden light—quite literally. The light bulbs were either gold themselves or filtered. There were two fireplaces, already aglow, and cookies were baking in an oven installed for this very purpose; the scent of sugar cookies was as important as the taste. The gallery had created a mixture of home and paradise. It wasn't real, of course. At the end of the evening, the lights would go off, the room would go cold.

But now, it was hiraeth. It was home.

Speaking of home, my mother was in town.

Why?

She and I were trained at giving each other space. Like, sometimes, half a planet's worth of space. She said she had some family business to talk over with me.

I was stumped.

My mormor, Mom's mother, had died several months ago. I'd seen Mom at the funeral, and she'd hugged me, but we hadn't really talked. I'd seen my aunts, uncles, and cousins. There was only one cousin I was close to: Reggie. Otherwise, I am solidly on the outskirts of the Nash family. So I didn't know what kind of family business I would be involved in.

It could, of course, just be personal business, hers and mine, but we each already had our own lives, with lots of space between us, as noted.

She didn't know much if anything about my life in Tranquility, and I liked it that way. Part of the rising panic (and it was beginning to feel like panic) was due to the vulnerability that would come with her knowing my intimate acquaintances, my friends, the man I loved, the magic of my residence and of my neighbors. All of it.

At least my best friend, Hannah Bricksford, the pastor of a local church I did not attend, was safely out of town.

Mom had already been to the Battened Hatch, so it was no longer a private safe space.

"Have any beer?" I looked up to find Brent Davis, our local newspaper editor, standing before me. "Never mind, I know you don't. I won't make you say it."

I smiled. "Next time, I'll remember to sneak in a Stella," I said, conspiratorially.

"Meanwhile, how about seltzer and lime. And, Avalon, I'd like you to meet Leonard Ruskin, Michael Michel's art consultant."

"Pleasure," said the gentleman beside him. He wore a brown and tan plaid jacket, white shirt, and a tan bow tie. He had a long face accented by wire rim glasses, under a shock of salt-and-pepper hair. The art expert from central casting—the perfect person to franchise all Michael Michel's calendars and prints, although tonight, he was undoubtedly helping the wealthy feel good about the purchase of multiple—and very large—paintings. He held out his hand and I shook it. "Can I get you a drink?"

"It's wisest not to when I'm working," he said.

"Another seltzer and lime?"

He nodded and I filled the order. "Where are you based?" I asked Mr. Ruskin.

"Maryland," he said. He offered a small salute with his glass and headed back into the reception. Manager Mona saw him, grabbed him by the arm, smiling sweetly, and steered him toward a well-heeled couple.

Brent remained, seemingly not in a hurry to chat up the glitterati. He was becoming a friend, someone I trusted. I should probably inform him...

"You know, I believe there's been a murder at MacTavish's."

He stood for a moment and took another sip of his drink. "Hunh," he said. "When?"

I gave him the approximate time. "Shelby should have heard it on the scanner," he said. He took out his phone and texted his newsroom editor.

"Yep," he said. "She's on it."

"Okay, good." I was surprisingly comforted that someone besides me was tired of death and not eager to jump headlong into the investigation. I did feel bad for the deceased, of course, but it seemed the best way for me to help would be to stay out of the way.

Near the end of the reception, I opened the last bottle of Champagne. I wondered if we could skate by on it for the last half hour, as bar traffic had slowed, but Mona appeared as I finished that first pour. Three glasses remained in the bottle. "It's your job to make sure we don't run out of anything. The next bottle must be chilled!" she exhorted.

"Sure," I said. "Where are they?"

"In the cellar!" She pointed a finger at a nondescript doorway behind the bar. "Lainie," she called. Her assistant magically appeared. For a moment I felt relief, assuming the assistant would handle the stairs, but this vanished along with Mona's next words. "You stay here and serve," she instructed, "while the bartender gets more bubbly."

And Mona moved back into the crowd.

Lainie looked at my cast, then gave me an apologetic shrug. She stayed put. I limped away. Mona was making sure I earned my pay.

The door opened to an old hallway with fraying tiles. Poorly lit, with low-wattage lightbulbs, it tore you away immediately from the golden light of the gallery. Straight at the end of the hallway was an EXIT sign with a push bar. Shortly before that was a metal door with a round silver doorknob, undoubtedly installed as a fire safety door in a previous decade.

I pushed it open and walked onto a wooden platform from which steps descended. The light switch was already turned on. Fortunately, the banister was solid. I clung to it and hopped the eight steps to the landing, then down the final eight. I had no idea how I would make it back up carrying a bottle of expensive Champagne.

Relieved to reach the stone floor at the bottom, I let myself sit on the stairs, stretching out the cast which chafed something awful. I scanned the room for the extra Champagne.

The first thing I saw were very tall, open wooden storage cages. They were simple constructions, two-by-fours stretching eight feet tall, boards on the top and bottom, and another set running around the middle. Inside were original paintings by Michael Michel, standing upright but leaning against each other. There were at least three of these long painting shelves, holding at least thirty or forty finished pieces of art. There were all sizes, from huge ones, ten by eight feet, down to the simpler three feet by two feet. Most of them were larger.

Alrighty, then.

The second thing I noticed were the rows of wine racks across the room. I wasn't close enough to see labels, but there seemed to be sections of reds, whites, and sparkling, stored on their sides. I'll admit I was curious about the collection.

The third thing was that behind the racks, the smooth walls were painted with pastoral scenes. Unlike the types sold by Mr. Michel, these were faded and old-fashioned, most likely painted by someone in generations past. I couldn't see much due to the storage racks, but one mural showed a cozy indoor scene: a comfy chair by a crackling fireplace, footrest and sleeping hound dog nearby, a book and a candle on a side table. Beneath it were two mouseholes with painted little doors, one open and one closed. A mouse stood outside one that was open revealing a candle and dinner table inside. The other door was closed, detailed with black iron hinges and a keyhole. Across from it was a hillside with children in old-fashioned clothing, girls in white ruffled dresses, boys in navy blue sailor suits with knee socks. They were on a hillside, flying multiple kites. The colors were faded, but I picked out orange, red, and green.

These scenes brought a different kind of hiraeth, a longing for another simpler time, one that was quixotic and fun and full of friends and laughter.

The fourth thing I saw was Leonard Ruskin, sitting in a green straight-backed chair with carved wooden feet and arm rests. "Oh, hi," I said, surprised. "I was sent for Champagne."

"Hello," he said. "I'm taking a breather."

We sat for a moment. "I had no idea Michael Michel was so prolific," I said. "It must help to have so much to offer."

"Ah, but one can't flood the market," he said. "It's all about timed release."

I nodded. "What's the story behind the painted walls?"

"They probably date from the late 1800s. That's why I'm down here. Communing with the spirit of someone who was idealistic back in the olden days."

"I'm enchanted by it, too," I said, careful not to say I wasn't so enchanted by Mr. Michel's work. "How can it still be so intact?"

"This is the perfect place to store wine and paintings. Cool and dry. What kind of Champagne do you need? Let's see if I can find it for you."

"Thanks. I'm also curious to take a look."

The bottles on the side facing the room were good wines, something you'd offer a client about to drop big money for a painting. On the other side, however, were bottles special enough to be meant solely for the owner. Although, as a bartender who'd served Michael, my guess was he okayed a budget and someone more in the know made the selections.

"Wow," I said. "Nice."

"Indeed."

We found the needed bottle and headed back to the stairs. Mr. Ruskin carried the bottle up for me. As we got to the top and opened the door to the hall, my phone rang. Apparently, I'd gotten a series of calls and texts in the time I'd been downstairs.

"I have to take this," I said.

"I'll drop off the bottle," he replied.

I leaned back against the wall and hit the answer button. "Nash!"

"Inspector Spaulding?"

"Where the hell are you?"

"I'm working an event. Why? Where are you?"

"Very funny. I'm at MacTavish's, wondering why you thought you could mosey on out."

"As I said, I'm working an event."

"You are top of the list of people we need to talk to about the murder."

"And why is that?"

"You know all those security cameras in the lobby? The ones that saw you sitting right next to the still-warm corpse?"

"I didn't kill him, Mike, you must have also seen that."

"You're the top of the witness list. Get back here ASAP."

"Send someone to the Welcome Home Gallery to pick me up in an hour. I've done as much walking as I can in a day."

"An hour. What were you thinking?" He hung up.

The bad news: I was involved with the murder, after all.

The good news: I took my phone and typed, *Mom, can we meet tomorrow? Turns out there was a murder at MacTavish's and I need to talk to the police.*

GOLDEN LIGHT

Ingredients

Sugar cookies (using your favorite recipe)
1 1/2 oz vanilla vodka
1 oz Amaretto
2 oz Baileys Irish Cream
1/2 oz heavy cream
Agave nectar (for rimming)
Ice
Cocktail shaker
Fine mesh cocktail strainer
Martini glass

Method

Place a few sugar cookies in a zip lock bag. Break them into crumbs and put onto small plate.
Squeeze agave nectar onto a small plate and dip martini glass to make sure the whole rim has nectar on it, then dip into cookies on the next plate. Set glass aside.
In cocktail shaker add ice, vodka, Baileys, Amaretto, and heavy cream. Shake all ingredients together. Strain into martini glass.

4

THE LADY VANISHES

Inspector Mike Spaulding of the state police awaited me in the security office behind the registration desk. With him was a younger officer who I recognized as Chris Newton. Newton was White, buzz haircut, perhaps three inches shorter than Spaulding, who was Black and in plain clothes. The most noticeable feature about Inspector Spaulding was that he wore a cast on his right leg. We'd jumped—dropped—from the same building during a recent murder investigation.

"You remember Newton?" he asked.

"I do."

They sat at a table, reviewing footage from the hotel's security cameras. The other officers had apparently moved on, as had Mac-Tavish's security guys, given the late hour.

"Do you need my statement?" I asked.

"Not technically. But an explanation would be nice." The word 'nice' was laced with irony.

Both men quit what they were doing and stared at me. Inspector Spaulding motioned me into the remaining chair. I sat and nodded at the screens they'd been watching. "What happened is exactly what it looks like. The gentleman in question was in the Battened Hatch having a drink—hot chocolate and bourbon. He said his name was Noel Schlessinger and he enjoyed attending gingerbread house competitions. The bar was busy. I didn't notice when he left. Sometime thereafter, Stormie Edwards, Pepper's sous chef, went to talk to him to see if he'd like to be interviewed for the show they're about to shoot for the Delicious Network, but he seemed impaired

29

and didn't answer her. She asked me to take a look. I did. He looked dead. I told her to inform security. I'm guessing she did."

"Why didn't you inform security?"

"Really? I had nothing to do with the situation and didn't want to become involved. I also didn't want to be late to the gallery opening. Have you met Mona, Michel's gallery manager? You'd think twice about being late, also."

Mike stared at me, then exhaled.

"Yeah, that's what it looked like," he said.

"So, who did it?" I asked, nodding toward the footage they'd been reviewing.

Inspector Spaulding nodded at Newton. He hit play on one of the camera feeds. The center lobby sprang to life in black and white. There was a clear shot of Noel Schlessinger seated on the banquette. Things seemed normal. It took a while to notice a young woman with bright red hair teased back behind a wide black headband. She wore a short white puffer jacket, a short red skirt and black leggings. She was sipping a cup of the free coffee offered in the lobby, and, while looking out the window, clocking the noise made by the hockey players. As she did, she nonchalantly backed into the room. As an extended group cheer went up, she turned, took the last steps towards Noel, and leaned in as if to speak to him. Instead, she removed a Luger with a silencer from her jacket, pressed it against the gingerbread man's heart, and pulled the trigger. She tugged Noel's jacket just enough to cover the spreading stain. The gun disappeared back into her jacket, a surprised look remaining on Schlessinger's face.

She stepped back and then sauntered toward the main doors across from the registration desk. As she reached it, the revolving door started spinning and a steady stream of new guests emerged into the lobby.

"Apparently the Delicious Network show sent a van up from New York City with some of the crew and contestants," Officer Newton said.

They'd pulled up at the exact moment the killer reached the area.

"Certainly there are other cameras?" I asked.

Taking his cue, Newton switched cameras to the outside view. We watched the van pull up and the riders descend. Several others straggled in. No one exited the hotel. No one.

"Then we've got this. Just beyond registration is a small hallway with a women's

and men's restrooms. There aren't cameras in that hall or in the restrooms, but even if she ducked into one, she'd have to leave sometime." Newton switched to the hallway that came off the lobby and the restrooms. "We won't make you watch it. But...no one comes through for a long time, and when guests finally do, none have a body type remotely similar to the assassin."

"The lady vanishes." I mused "You've checked the restrooms?"

"We found nothing. No escape windows. No abandoned wigs or Lugers," said Newton.

"It was obviously a hit and she was a pro. But even Houdini couldn't completely vanish into thin air," said Spaulding.

"Why would someone kill a guy who goes around the country attending gingerbread house contests?"

"No one would," said Newton.

"Hunh," I said.

"We've got to get back to the barracks," said Spaulding. Then, to his junior officer: "Go ahead and call the night security person back in, then pull around the car."

Newton complied, pulling on his jacket and shutting the door behind him.

"Walk with me," Mike said, inclining his head towards me.

"Limping acceptable?"

"I cannot wait to get this damn thing off," he responded.

We left the security office in the hands of Menninger, who made sure all the CCTV feeds were current.

Mike and I hobbled together towards the entrance. The attendant pulled the non-revolving door open for us and we emerged into the chilly night air.

"I have something for you," Inspector Spaulding said under his breath. He shoved a rectangular box into my hand. It was emblazoned with a photo of some sort of electronic device.

"What is it?"

"A personal locator beacon," he said. "Actually, two of them. They're for finding people when there's no phone service or if they're out in the mountains. We got a bunch in at headquarters. I've given a few to people I'm close to."

Aww, so we were friends.

"Or people who go dashing off into dangerous situations without thinking."

Or, that.

"Are you allowed to give them out?"

"If you move or I get transferred, please return it."

"Okay, will do." I stuffed it into my bartender bag. "Although I'm officially taking it easy."

"Do you have a way to get home?"

I nodded to my cast, thinking how much it sucked not being able to drive. "It's why God invented Uber."

"Okay. See you."

"See you."

I briefly wondered if Mom was still awake. But I was beat, certainly not ready for any talk about family stuff.

I texted Jeff, a local cabbie, now a friend. He arrived quickly.

"Home?" he asked.

"You know me too well," I said.

He jumped out of the SUV and crossed in front to open the front passenger's side door. Then he stood for a moment, his head cocked. "Do you feel that?"

"Feel what?"

"The air. Something different. Snow is coming."

"Not according to the weather app."

"Hmm."

It was nearly midnight when he dropped me off in the private glen where I lived. He'd been running a tab for me since I got my cast. I settled up. He blinked his lights as a farewell and I headed up, past my landlord's large log cabin, up the hill and over the footbridge up to my cottage. The back porch light was on, as was the kitchen light, which meant Philip, my boyfriend, was in bed. Sometimes he had international phone calls in the morning he had to be wide awake for.

His Pomeranian, Whistle, heard me come in. She'd jumped off our bed and come into the kitchen to get me. I let her out for a final time, and on her return, I picked her up and held her close. Her fur was fluffy and she was warm. She licked my face, settled in happily when I placed her back onto the bed next to the sleeping form of Philip. I changed in the bathroom and came back to snuggle under the covers.

Philip roused sleepily. "Crazy day? Lots to tell me?"

"And how."

"Me, too. Hideaway?" It was our code for hiding away from the world, getting a good night's sleep, and starting fresh in the morning.

"Yes, please." Philip opened his arms and I burrowed in against his chest. He kissed the top of my head—and proceeded to fall back to sleep, gentle snores starting almost immediately. Many people find their partners' snoring annoying, and I probably would find window-rattling snores to be so. But I'd come to count on Philip's as my own personal white noise.

Was our imaginary hideaway strong enough to block out death and the primal place a mother holds in our lives? Would it work to get me through the night?

Half an hour later, as I descended the ladder into unconsciousness, a stray thought hit.

I disengaged from Philip and sat up. Then I stood and went into the living room.

The truth was, I wasn't able to get the murder out of my head. If the assassin hadn't left the hotel, it meant she was still there. Did she have unfinished business to complete? Who was the gingerbread man really? Why was he in town? What kind of threat did he pose, one that merited a bullet through the chest?

Dear God, of all times for Mom to be in town. Staying at Mac-Tavish's.

As I sat on the couch, watching the landscape by moonlight diffused by clouds, it began to snow.

THE LADY VANISHES

Ingredients

Cocktail
3 pints fresh raspberries (set 1 pint aside for garnish)
Lemonade
1 lemon for zest
2 cups sugar
3 cups water
1 ½ oz lemon vodka
Lemon bitters
Fine mesh cocktail strainer
Cocktail shaker
Ice
Citrus zester
Nick and Nora glass

Meringue

2 egg whites
1 cup sugar
Medium saucepan
Mixing bowl
Whisk

Method

Meringue

Create a Bain-Marie with a medium pot filled with two inches of water and mixing bowl. Add the egg whites and sugar to the bowl and whisk continuously over medium heat, making sure that the water in the pot does not touch the bowl.

Whisk until mixture steams for about 4 minutes and is a creamy texture while ensuring that sugar is dissolved. Remove from heat and add to mixer with a whisk attachment and whisk until you have soft white fluffy peaks. Set aside and make cocktail.

Cocktail

In medium saucepan, add water, raspberries, and sugar over medium heat. Stir
until the raspberries have broken down. Take off heat and set aside. When cool, strain raspberry mix to remove seeds.

In cocktail shaker, add ice, lemon vodka, 2 ounces of the raspberry liquid, 2 oz of lemonade, and a few dashes of lemon bitters. Shake and strain into martini glass. Add a dollop of meringue to glass and top with the zest of a fresh lemon.

5

THE GANG'S ALL HERE

THE NEXT MORNING, I left the cottage before Philip woke up. I didn't have enough of a handle on the murder to explain it to anyone else. Not to mention, I didn't want him to know my mother was in town. I'd already planned how I'd introduce Philip to my mom: in twenty years, when he and I lived in Paris and she was changing planes at Orly. Philip and I would go out to the airport and wave at her through the security gate.

It had snowed perhaps half an inch. The roads and sidewalks were clear, the cold ground covered with enough white to look elegant. Fortunately, Jeff was already on call. He was only slightly smug about his prediction of the snow.

To my surprise, even though it was morning and the Battened Hatch wasn't open, the place was humming. Had I told Stormie she could use my pub as a production hub for the gingerbread competition?

I did not remember doing so. And yet, surprise! Here was everybody.

There was a fellow bringing in tiers of lights from a van outside. It made sense for them to hire local sound and lighting people. There was a woman in colorful, flowing Bohemian dress standing with an assistant, moving a man's face this way and that. I assumed she was the make-up team lead and he was a participant.

"Who's in charge? Who's in charge?" A woman wearing a German-style dirndl marched in through the hallway. Her blouse was white, the lace-up vest black and sewn with flowers. Her skirt was black and the apron red. Even her accent was German. She was maybe forty, her light brown hair boasting a blunt cut at chin length. She was someone whose presence made itself felt.

Yet I echoed her sentiment. Who was in charge?

I went behind the bar and pushed through the door to the kitchen. It was swarming with activity. Apparently, all the gingerbread participants were being treated to a free buffet breakfast in Pepper's, while tourists had the option of ordering fancy stuff off the menu, sending the kitchen into overdrive.

"Where's Stormie?" I asked one of the line cooks. He nodded back toward the door into Pepper's. Diners, becoming brighter and perkier with every cup of coffee, were there. Stormie was not.

I headed into the lobby and saw her by the entrance to the hallway which led back to the large rooms used for meetings, or in this instance, cookie house creation. She was on the phone, looking distressed. Today's chef coat was dark blue with a double row of buttons. It looked both stylish and professional.

"Let me know if you can get a plane out," she was saying. She clicked the phone off and stood for a moment, regaining her composure.

I stood next to her. "What's up?" Honestly, she seemed almost as upset as she had been when she thought Schlessinger was dead.

"That was the producer. He was supposed to arrive this morning, but his flight is cancelled in Chicago. Snow and high winds. He's hoping the storm will pass and he can get into New York City, though he's fairly sure he won't be able to get up here. He says he can oversee things from the city... if he can get there."

"Yikes," I said. "Who is on the ground who can lead the troops?" She looked at me. I rephrased. "Who is running the show?"

"They hired as much local crew as possible—lighting, make-up, camera. There's a director they've used before, a Will Acton, but I haven't seen him. He was supposed to be here last night."

"Did you call, my lady?" A short, wiry, intense man came up to us. He had a narrow face with a day's bristle under curly salt-and-pepper hair. He wore tight jeans and an open-collared shirt. "Will

Acton, at your service. I was exploring our space. Considering the patina. It all starts with the patina."

"Oh," said Stormie. "Well, good. Everyone's meeting in the pub—" and, to me, "Marta said we could." Back to Will, "In any case, you'll want to go and talk to everyone, I'm sure, since baking starts tonight."

"Heading there now."

As the director left, I turned to Stormie. "I wonder if the snow's headed this way from Chicago," I said. "If so, I guess it's good every-one's here."

"Except Tomie. The producer. Oh, and I haven't seen Darla West, the host from the Delicious Network."

"I know everything's set up, but even if something goes terribly wrong and it has to be cancelled or postponed, in the grand scheme of things, it is just a gingerbread house contest."

Stormie looked at me, stricken.

"Sorry," I said. "I know it means a lot to the contestants and the Delicious Network. But...why are *you* talking to the producer? Why is it your concern?"

"Tomie is my boyfriend. This is the first thing they've asked him to produce by himself."

"But a snowstorm isn't his fault..."

"This is his big chance. He's earned it. And we've worked so hard."

"I get it." And I did. It explained why Stormie had coordinated having the contest here, at MacTavish's. How fortuitous it was to be able to film when Chef Angelica was away.

Stormie gave a wry smile and headed back to the kitchen. So, Marta had given permission to use the Battened Hatch. She was my assistant manager, and she could make decisions when I was not available. I checked my phone. No texts. She hadn't checked to see if I was available.

Okay. I took a breath and headed back to the Hatch.

I arrived just as Will Acton was finishing his welcome remarks.

From the scattered applause, I assumed the remarks he'd delivered weren't as stirring as say, Henry the Fifth's St. Crispin's Day speech. The crowd broke. Acton headed for the lighting guy.

"The patina? What is this patina?" asked the contestant in the German dirndl, to no one in particular. She turned to me and thrust out her hand. "Gretl Haus. What refrigerator do I use?"

Stormie swung in from the kitchen. I pointed at her, though I felt bad doing so. How could she be expected to run the kitchen and co-ordinate the shoot with MacTavish's space? Where was the production coordinator? *Was* there a production coordinator?

Where was Marta, who was apparently offering up our space? I thought I saw her in conversation at a booth, but before I could head over, there was a light tap on my shoulder.

"Excuse me?"

The voice was breathy and timid. Before me stood a young girl, early teens, white tee covered by a red plaid shirt. Her dark brown hair was straight, her teeth lined with braces.

"I'm Emelia Culver. I'm so excited to be here," she said. "Where do I go?"

"I wish I knew." I was about to move away when I saw the look on Emelia's face. She said she was excited. She was terrified.

"How old are you? Are you here by yourself?"

"I'm fourteen. My great-grandad was supposed to come. He's from here. He couldn't wait. But he had a stroke last week."

"I am so sorry to hear that! I'm sure they would have understood if you hadn't come."

"He said this was his greatest wish, that I do this. I have a cousin twice removed who lives around here. I'm going to call her to be my chaperone. I'm so excited."

She looked ready to cry.

At that moment, Marta looked up from her intense conversation in booth three and saw me. I motioned her over. She regretfully broke away. As she did, I saw who she was talking to.

Mom.

Of course. Here we go again.

"Marta, this is Emelia. She is a contestant. She is here by herself. As you know, we open in less than an hour and we have to get ready. But can you find someone who can tell Emelia what to do?"

"Thank you," the teen said. "Thank you." She went to pick up her carry bag.

"You told them they could use our space?" I asked Marta.

"Stormie was overseeing. I thought she'd discussed it with you."

"You were talking to my mom? What about?"

Marta's eyes shone. "Yeah. She's so smart! And she doesn't look at you like you're crazy when you ask what she thinks about things like the unidentified aerial phenomena, you know, what they call UFOs, nowadays. I mean, there really are flying craft with technology beyond our capabilities. Even Congress has admitted as much. So, what are they? What does it all mean?"

Dear God. "What did she say?"

"First, she quoted Arthur C. Clark: 'Either we're alone in the universe or we are not. Both are equally terrifying.' Then she said there's so much we don't understand, but we're discovering more every day. She says she thinks we'll once again find out we're not the center of the universe, and it will cause as much upheaval as when Galileo said the same thing."

"Marta?" Young Emelia was back.

"Hi, come on. The production coordinator is named Esther Ringwald. She's over here." She pointed toward a woman with a petite physique and red hair pulled back into a ponytail. Marta and Emelia headed her way.

I stared. Red hair. Petite. Could it be? Was the assassin really still here? But even if she was, she would have changed her hair—been wearing a wig—certainly?

My waitstaff was arriving to prepare for opening. If the ginger-bread people hadn't moved on in a few minutes, I'd talk to the production coordinator myself. She couldn't be the assassin. Why would a cooking show crew member kill a gingerbread aficionado, and then stick around? Made no sense.

Someone put a hand on my right shoulder and I jumped.

I turned to find Philip Young, my Philip, standing close behind me.

"What's going on?" he asked, amused by the pandemonium.

"A gingerbread house contest. Being filmed for the Delicious Network. Come." I took his hand and led him out of the hubbub, disappearing once again into the storeroom. "Sorry I left before you woke up," I said. "I'm trying to deal with... all this." I swept an arm to indicate everyone, everywhere.

"Hey," he said. "Take a breath."

I turned to him, and he put his arms around me, his chin resting protectively on top of my head. I took a breath. Everything felt better. He was that kind of person. One who really cared and listened and told you why he appreciated you. When things got away from him—as they had lately—he had descended into a dark place, into himself and his art, it really threw me. I was glad he was back.

Philip is a painter. Non-representational, usually. I met him when he was repainting rooms at the hotel. He's the one who painted my cast. He paints lots of stuff, I guess. The thought made me smile.

His grandfather was a well-known artist from India and Philip spent a lot of time there. His skin was light brown and smooth to the touch, his hair jet-black, thick with a slight curl if he didn't comb it out.

"And somebody got murdered here yesterday. In the lobby," I said.

"Really? That would explain the crime tape around the settee."

"The murderer was a slight woman with red hair. I'm trying to believe she's not still here."

"Even if she was, do you need to worry? Why would she kill you?"

"Why would she kill some guy who goes to gingerbread house contests?"

"Got me there."

"You said you had some stuff going on, too." I looked around. "You know what? I'm going to get chairs, a floor lamp, and a rug for the back of the room. But you were saying? Stuff going on?"

"Yeah. You remember I told you my main mentor was angry and telling galleries to pull my work?"

"I still can't believe that." Philip had studied in Paris and one of his teachers was steering his career.

"He had his reasons."

"What? What were they? Reasons to betray someone?"

Philip sighed. "You know my dad is an artists' rep. We've never worked together. Frankly, I was young and unestablished, and neither of us ever brought it up. But then, a gallery owner friend of his in Paris needed some new artists and Dad talked me into giving the gallerist some paintings. Meanwhile, my mentor thought *he* had complete control of where my work was. He was furious. He told the galleries he works with to quit carrying me. I think I have to go see him."

"Will you remove your work from the gallery your dad supports?"

"It might be too late even if I do. And... it's the first time my father had really asked me for anything. That's why I feel I've got to go. I've got to talk to people, face to face. Or my career is over before it even truly begins."

I hugged him. How I wanted to fix things. "Cheer up," I said. "Maybe you can be like Van Gogh or El Greco and become filthy rich after you die."

"Everyone I need to talk to is in Paris now. I'm going to fly out as soon as I can."

"I understand." And I did. I didn't mention courage began seeping from my heart in droplets when I contemplated him being gone.

"Let me know when your flight is – and and check the weather. It seems there's a front moving this way."

"I will." He released me.

"Oh," I said. "Something else."

He stopped and turned back. With him here, at MacTavish's, the information was bound to come out.

"My mom."

"What about her?" Needless to say, he'd heard a thing or two from me about our relationship.

"She's kind of... here."

"What?"

"She kind of showed up. There's a family matter or something."

"Where is she now?"

"Booth three."

"Holy Carolina Reaper, Av," he said. "Talk about burying the lede! Why didn't you tell me?"

"I...have plans for when you two meet. In twenty years. When we're living in Paris."

He smiled. "Which arrondissement?" He looked into my eyes and saw I was serious. "So, do you want me to steer clear?"

"Would you?"

"Your mother, Anna Nash, is sitting in booth three and you want me to not meet her."

"You can meet her."

"But not tell her I'm living with her daughter?"

"Maybe yes, don't?"

"You'd prefer I didn't even say hello."

I nodded, miserable.

"Why?"

"Because if you do, you'll become one of her acolytes. She's funny and smart and interested in what you're interested in. I will cease to exist in your universe except as her daughter."

"But supposing what I'm interested in is her daughter?"

"One of her best topics. Same deal. And you'll leave the conversation asking me what my problem is—can't I see how wonderful she is?"

"Okay," he said. "Twenty years, in Paris, it is."

I grinned and shoved him toward the door. He stopped short of it, grabbed me again, and kissed me. "I'll let you know when I book a flight."

Back in the pub, the Gingerbread House folks had cleared out. Except one. Gretl Haus came roaring in from the street door and screeched to a halt in front of me. "Where did they all go? I had to make a call! Where are they?"

"I believe they're in Ballroom One," Philip said. "I know where it is. I can walk you there."

"I'm not used to being treated—"

"While we walk, could you tell me about your dirndl? Is it from a specific place? Do the colors have meaning?"

This caught her off guard. "Why, yes, they do."

Philip put an arm around her shoulders and steered her toward the lobby door. As he did, he looked over at booth three, where he had a partial view of Mom as she worked on papers from a file folder in front of her. He looked at me and winked. Then he and Gretl left.

My crew was now ready to open. Things were under control. I could put it off no longer. I went over and slid in across from Mom. "Good morning," I said. "Sorry about last night. I am free after work today, for sure."

She looked up and smiled. "That would be great," she said. She wore a burnt orange shirt, its navy-blue stripe through one side of the collar pulling it together with her jeans. Her hair was pulled back into a ponytail and she wore reading glasses—the complete Superwoman disguise. It didn't begin to work.

"Are those?"

She nodded to the file. "Yeah. Papers from Mom's estate."

I forget sometimes that my mormor was her mother. While I'd lost my beloved grandmother, she'd lost her mom. A primal thing, the bonds between mothers and daughters.

Apparently.

"Can I get you some coffee?" I asked. "Or some breakfast? Fruit and yogurt?" She was a vegetarian. Not the eggs and bacon type.

"You know what? That would be great. Is it okay if I sit here until you need the booth?"

"Sure. As long as you'd like."

I went and asked the kitchen to make up a very nice fruit and yogurt parfait. "Is it for your mom?" whispered the line cook. Word was out.

As I returned to the floor, two people came through the hallway from the lobby: Inspector Mike Spaulding and a woman I didn't recognize.

"Avalon Nash, this is Jules Eckhardt, a friend of mine who teaches at John Jay College of Criminal Justice. Visiting the area." Jules' hair was brown and shoulder-length. She wore black pants, and a blue-striped white shirt under a cobalt blue sweater. Her glasses were brown, the frames so wide they seemed to be making an 'I am an academic' kind of statement. We nodded at each other.

"Do you have a moment?"

I said yes and felt surprised when Inspector Spaulding told his guest he'd be back with her shortly. I headed for the bar and he followed me over.

"What's up?" I said when we were out of earshot. Then, because I couldn't help it, "Do you think the killer is still here? If she was, she wouldn't still have red hair, would she, like the production coordinator? I mean, any assassin worth her salt knows to use wigs. And why would she kill a gingerbread house aficionado?"

"Number one, I don't know. Perhaps. Number two, still don't know. Usually, if you commit a crime looking easily recognizable—sporting a distinctive hair color, wearing an unusual hat or outfit – you change your look right away. But again, I don't know.

"Number three, Schlessinger may have been a gingerbread house aficionado, I can't say. But our deceased was not hard to track down.

It's safe to say he was here working his other job. Which raises more
questions than it answers."

THE GANG'S ALL HERE

Ingredients

1 ½ oz mezcal
Smoky flavored bitters
1 fresh pineapple
2 ½ oz of fresh pineapple juice
2 pints of fresh blackberries
1 egg white
Ice
Cocktail shaker
Rocks glass

Method

Cut a third of the pineapple into slices about a quarter inch thick, leaving the skin on. Grill to get a nice char. Cut the rest into chunks without skin and put into juicer or blender. Make juice and set aside.
Juice the blackberries separately.
In cocktail shaker add ice, mezcal, egg white, and pineapple juice, and shake ingredients until you have a nice froth. Pour into rocks glass. Add extra ice if needed.
Use a cocktail spoon to slowly add the blackberry juice to the top so you have a nice layer of juice resting on top of the cocktail.
Finish cocktail by adding a dash of smoky bitters, a piece of grilled pineapple and a few fresh blackberries.

6

COVERING THE BASES

"HIS OTHER JOB?" I repeated, staring blankly at Inspector Spaulding.

"He was a bounty hunter. Noel Schlessinger was indeed his real name. He wasn't hiding. So. Who was he after? And, more to the point, who wanted to stop him?"

Noel Schlessinger, the guy sitting here yesterday drinking a bourbon hot chocolate, was Boba Fett?

"How do we find out who he was after?"

"We have people in Ossining looking through his office there. Also, the head of HR at MacTavish's has okayed a background check on the current employees."

I must have looked offended, as Mike said, "Why? What would they find?"

"Nothing on me," I said quickly. "Well, nothing interesting. It just seems a bit invasive."

"Most employees had background checks run when they were hired. I'm not expecting to turn up anything untoward. Just covering all the bases."

"Thanks for letting me know. This is becoming more complicated."

"Murders so often are."

It was approaching lunchtime and the Battened Hatch was open but not yet busy. Manuela, our senior waitperson, went to table three, where Mike Spaulding's bespectacled friend Jules was currently seated in deep conversation with my mother. Of course. To my surprise, both women ordered lunch and continued their tête-à-tête.

As Mike moved away, Marta appeared at my side. "So? What's up?"

"Walk with me."

I gave Manuela a sign we'd be right back. I steered Marta out and through the lobby. Once we were out of earshot, I filled her in on the latest about the Gingerbread Man.

"He was a bounty hunter?" she asked. "Like Din Djarin?" Same Star Wars saga, different generations.

"Yup."

Curiosity about the cooking competition led me through the back meeting halls, to the ballrooms where the shoot would take place. The folding wall between ballrooms A and B was pulled back, giving enough room for six workstations and all the filming equipment.

A few years ago, some civic group hosted a Yule Ball at Mac-Tavish's. The festively painted flats they used had been brought out of storage to provide a backdrop of a cheerful holiday cottage, complete with Christmas tree, Menorah, and fake snow falling outside the windows.

"Wow," said Marta. "They've been busy."

The six bakers' workstations stood ready as the lighting technician and his assistant hung rows of lights from an overhead bar. Each contestant had claimed a table and was now arranging their tools and ingredients, preparing to create their culinary masterpieces.

Director Will Acton stood arguing with the camera operator. "We need snow in the frame! Snow! This is a winter fantasy!"

"Tell them to add it in post."

"No. I must have it. Get someone on a ladder! It's not that hard."

As their dispute continued, Marta and I turned back to our actual jobs. As we did, Emilia noticed us and rushed over. "I can't find her," she said, waving her phone. "My second cousin. I'm not sure my great-grandpa even told her I was coming. I don't know what to do. If they find out I'm here underage without a chaperone, they'll send me home."

"Oh, no," I said.

"Could you?" Emilia was looking at Marta. She took her hand and tugged on it, pleadingly. "We're allowed to have a helper to make the house. Could you be my helper? And my guardian? You're eighteen, right?"

"Yes."

I admit I loved this. I was used to thinking of Marta as the young'un, looking for guidance. The times, they were a-changin'.

"Would you help me, please? I'm doing a Treasure Island gingerbread house—well, pirate ship. Could you help?"

Marta looked at me, her boss. Oh, for pity's sake. I pulled her a few steps away. "Do you want to?" I asked. She nodded.

"Okay." The contest would be over in a couple of days—one of which was Marta's day off, anyway. "It's up to you."

"Text me if you get busy," she said.

The relief on Emelia's face was profound. "Come over. I'll show you the steps."

Thus I returned to the pub with one fewer employee than I left with.

An hour into lunch, a familiar-looking businessman walked in. His silvering hair was slicked and combed. He wore a perfectly tailored grey suit, crisp white shirt, and silk tie. He exuded intelligence and well-to-do-ness.

"Hi, Avalon," he said. "I need a table where I can have a lunch meeting. Somewhere as private as possible."

Though he looked familiar, I wasn't sure how he knew my name. He saw the confusion on my face. "What? You don't recognize me without the plaid suit and bowtie?"

It dawned on me. The man from the wine cellar. "Mr. Ruskin? No, I didn't recognize you."

"There are many layers to my job. Sometimes, I need to look like someone you'd trust to help you pick out a painting by Michael

Michel. Other times, Cézanne. Different clientele. Different wardrobe."

"Got it. The booths tend to be more private. We're clearing one now. Would that work?" Our booths have wooden backs that extend well above the heads of seated patrons.

"Yes, thanks."

As we stood there a moment, waiting, I wondered who in Tranquility could afford a Cézanne. The question was answered shortly after Mr. Ruskin sat down and was joined by Planton Cavalleros, billionaire and patriarch of a prominent Spanish family who summered in Tranquility. His son Tomás was a good friend of Philip's. They'd been roommates in Paris when they studied painting together. The first time I'd visited the Cavalleros mansion, I was bartending a birthday bash. The second time, I was with Philip as a guest of Tomás. The house was across Lake Tranquility, which was located in the town next to Tranquility itself. Well, both 'house' and 'mansion' undersell it. The abode was kind of the size of a small country, but snazzier.

It held a soft spot in my heart, as it was the first place Philip and I made love.

In any case, this was the first time Mr. Cavalleros had dined at the Battened Hatch, to my knowledge. His outfit was fashionable, while also looking like he'd awakened and pulled on any old thousand-dollar shirt he found in his closet. His charm and power were innate and effortless.

I welcomed both men with a smile and handed them the menus, informing them Manuela would be their server.

Then I took a step back, which brought me into the space in front of booth three. As I did, Chef Stormie exited the kitchen and made a beeline for me. What now?

She held out a photo of a well-dressed, well-coiffed woman who looked the part of a television presenter. "Darla West *can't come*!" she hissed.

"Your host?"

"Yes! From the Delicious Network!" At that moment, Stormie looked up and saw Anna Nash somehow miraculously apparated in front of her. You could see the grist mill of her thoughts beginning to turn.

It was clear both women in the booth had heard Stormie's pronouncement. Stormie continued, "One of the most famous hosts from the Delicious Network was supposed to host the competition! She's stuck in Kansas City!"

She paused, likely working up the courage to ask Mom directly.

Mom smiled her warm smile. "I'm sorry for your predicament, Chef," she said with sincere empathy. "I'm sorry I can't step in for you. I'll be gone long before the show has finished shooting. And my agent." She shook her head. "I wouldn't sic her on you. On anybody. Trust me."

It was the kindest turn-down. Mom was good at that. Stormie hadn't actually asked, so she hadn't truly been turned down. And Mom had respected her by calling her "chef."

Stormie grabbed my arm and dragged me back toward the bar. "Who is camera-ready that you can think of who lives local? Who can we get to fill in?"

"I'll put on my thinking cap. But most of the celebrities I know are out of town at the moment."

She dropped my arm and spoke more quietly. "What did the inspector tell you?"

"Gingerbread Man was a bounty hunter. They're running a background check on all hotel employees to see if there's anyone working here who might have skipped bail and have a bounty on them."

Stormie burst out laughing, then caught herself. She returned to the kitchen, shaking her head, her shoulders bobbing with mirth in spite of her best efforts.

Not the reaction I expected.

It was maybe half an hour later that Philip stopped back by. He owned a craftsman-style home near the Battened Hatch which housed his studio and other items he'd not yet moved over to my place. I could tell he was coming from there because he was carrying an empty suitcase and wearing his Paris coat, a long woolen plaid print jacket that looked good with the brown turtleneck underneath it. It was decidedly too much for Tranquility but was perfect for the European art scene. I smiled at the French version of my man.

"What's up?" I asked.

"Looks like I'll be able to fly out tonight on the nine o'clock commuter plane to Boston. I should be gone less than a week."

"I hope everything goes well. It doesn't seem right that the two men who care about and admire you most have put you in this position."

"They each feel they have ownership of my career and want to assert it," he said. "The problem is, I do owe them both."

"But when their demands overlap..."

"Pray for me now and at the hour of my death," he said with a smile.

Philip travelled a good deal. For some reason, this was the first time I'd ever wanted to hold on to him and plead, "Don't go."

It had been that kind of day.

And it apparently wasn't over. A rustling from the lobby doorway caught our attention. Nelson, the hotel's head of security, entered the restaurant with Officer Joe Cooper of the Tranquility police department. They stood for a moment, scanning the establishment.

What now?

They continued their visual sweep of the room, until they spotted the women at booth three. Together, the tall security man in black slacks and jacket and the local cop walked purposefully toward them.

You've got to be kidding me.

It was one thing for me to have to deal with the peculiarities of Tranquility, but my mom did not deserve to.

By the time they'd arrived at the booth, I had, too.

"Ms., uh, Karenina?" asked Nelson.

Mom looked up, surprised.

"We need to have a word with you."

"Yes?"

"Is there somewhere we can go?"

"This is fine," said Mom quietly. "We can speak in sotto voce."

The men looked at each other. Nelson gave it a go. "I'm sorry to inform you," he said in a hearty whisper, "that a member of our waitstaff visited your room a short time ago to deliver a Champagne bucket and cheese board, sent by management."

Really? MacTavish's sends people wine and cheese boards? News to me.

"Nice," said Mom. "Thank you."

"Unfortunately, after knocking, the waiter entered the room to find an unclothed man sitting at the table by the bed. When he found it wasn't you, he got very angry and made threatening moves toward her."

"Is she all right?"

"Yes. She dropped the heavy items she was carrying and escaped the room" Officer Cooper said. "To be clear, you weren't expecting to be joined by any such gentleman?"

COVERING THE BASES

Ingredients

1 ½ oz vodka
½ oz coffee liquor
2 oz kefir
1 egg white
½ simple syrup
Pinch of each ground up; cinnamon, clove, ginger, and
cumin (reserve a little on side to
dust over cocktail for garnish)
Ice
Cocktail shaker
Cocktail strainer
Coupe glass

Method

In cocktail shaker add ice, simple syrup, vodka, coffee
liquor, kefir, egg white and dried
Spices. Shake until cocktail is nice and frothy. Strain into
coupe glass and dust a little
bit of dried spices to finish the cocktail.

7

THE NAKED TRUTH

"No. No, I wasn't. Did you catch him?"

"Unfortunately, by the time we got there, he had departed."

Nelson reached into his pocket and produced a short security camera video depicting one of the rear doors to a parking lot. A lean, sinewy, naked man, holding a pile of clothing topped by a pair of shoes, ran out of the door and unlocked a car with a key fob. He got in, sitting on what must have been a very chilly driver's seat, fired the car to life, and screeched toward the exit.

"Have you ever met him?"

"Never had the pleasure," said Mom. "I'm sure I'd recognize that—well, I don't recognize any part of him."

While she seemed lighthearted, a heavy lead ball dropped from my heart to my stomach. Our society teaches us to desire fame, but it's poison in so many ways. Not least of which is when it lures men to sit naked in your hotel room waiting to rape you.

Nelson said, "The hotel is pleased to move you to another room, one perhaps more easily guarded."

"However," Officer Cooper broke in, "It's our sincere recommendation that you move to another location until the perpetrator is caught. Do you have somewhere to stay?"

"Yes," I blurted. "Yes, she does."

As Nelson made a plan to go with Mom back to her room to pack her things, Philip moved closer to me. "Where are you thinking she'll stay? Our place isn't exactly secure. If anyone knows she's there, it would be easy to sneak onto the property and over to the house. You remember when Gran was afraid people might discover her, she paid to have security by the property entrance. We don't have that."

"So," I said, thinking as fast as I could. "Do you have any ideas?"

"Give me a minute."

I moved closer to booth three. "I'll help get your stuff," I said.

"Thanks," Mom said.

She turned to Professor Eckhardt. "I've enjoyed our conversation."

"As have I."

"Let's stay in touch."

Jules Eckhardt stood and shook Mom's hand. She grabbed her coat and headed for the lobby door.

I looked up to see Philip at the next table, talking earnestly to Planton.

He nodded and came back over to me.

"Planton Cavalleros has invited your mom to stay at his place."

Mom looked up at us.

"This is getting more interesting," she said. "First, who is Planton Cavalleros? And who is the gentleman who got me the invitation?"

Philip realized his time was at hand, like it or not. He smiled, stepped up and offered his hand. "I'm Philip. Friend of Avalon's."

Mom extended her and they shook warmly. "Anna Nash. Mom of Avalon."

"I'm also a friend of the Cavalleros family," Philip said.

Officer Cooper's light grey eyebrows shot up, as if he was recalibrating his opinion of Philip's status around here. "Well," he said, in a crusty, officer voice. "If you can stay there, that should be safe."

"The only way to get to it is by boat," Philip explained to Mom. "And it's alarmed to kingdom come."

"True," I said. "I've been locked out of it, myself."

Mom smiled at Nelson and Cooper. "I appreciate your help, gentlemen. Let me talk to my daughter. I'll find you in the lobby, Mr. Nelson, in a few minutes. To get my stuff."

They nodded, expressions underlining the seriousness with which they viewed the situation.

To my surprise, Marta had returned. She stood by the bar, unabashedly staring at Mom and me and Philip and the police officer. I limped over as fast as I could. "You're back?"

"Yeah. I signed on as Emelia's guardian and we got stuff organized. She won't need me until she bakes her gingerbread. They gave her the 1 a.m. slot."

Ah, yes. Baking in the kitchen overnight to be well out by breakfast in the hopes Chef Angelica would never know.

"Could you possibly close tonight?" I asked.

"What's going on?"

"Some jerk broke into Mom's hotel room, lying in wait. Luckily, they delivered Champagne and he bolted when he saw the room service woman."

"We deliver Champagne?"

I responded with an *I know, right?* look.

"Yes, I can close," she said.

"Thank you very much."

I returned to Mom as security left.

"What do you think?" she asked me. "Should I go to the place across the lake?"

"It would probably be smart," I admitted. Then, to Philip, "Do you think Planton would let me come over to get her settled, if there would be a boat coming back later tonight?"

He went to ask.

That way we'd have some time together to talk, and in a neutral setting, which might make things easier.

Philip returned. "Planton and his friend are about to head that way now. The friend, the fellow he's talking to now, will return this evening. Planton would be happy to have you accompany your mom."

I gave his hand a squeeze of gratitude.

"Say, can you pick up my black jacket when you're there? I think I left it in Tomás' living room."

"Sure."

I went with Philip to speak to Planton and Mr. Ruskin, who said they'd be leaving in about twenty minutes. They'd pick us up at a side door and give us a ride to the dock.

Then I went with Mom to pull her belongings together. I'll admit that doing so had me a bit shaken. Wasn't it enough that we had a killer likely still among us? Did Mom have to be here now, and did we need to add a stalker to the mix?

"Thanks for coming," she said to me as we followed Nelson to her guest room. She'd booked just a regular room in the middle of a regular hall. Nelson was right. It wasn't the safest choice.

But if you didn't know who your perpetrators were, was any-where safe?

THE NAKED TRUTH

Ingredients

½ oz Absinthe
1 oz Gin
4 oz chilled sparkling white wine
3 oz. orange blossom water
Pinch of raw sugar
Fresh orange peel for zest and garnish
Ice
Cocktail shaker
Champagne flute

Method

Add a pinch of raw sugar to the bottom of the
Champagne flute.
In cocktail shaker add ice, orange blossom water,
absinthe, and gin. Shake until chilled then strain into
flute. Finish cocktail by slowly pouring chilled sparkling
white wine to the top.
Take a fresh orange peel and wipe around the rim of the
Champagne flute and twist over the top of the flute to
release some of the natural orange oils over cocktail.

8

THE LOST ART

ONCE AGAIN, I attempted to absent myself from hit persons and gingerbread. This time by boarding a large boat and cruising across Lake Tranquility with my mother.

It was off season, to say the least, and we were one of the only crafts on the water. The November sky was sunlit with occasional puffs of cloud, but a larger bank of them seemed to be rallying to the west. Mom and I sat on comfortable cushions in an enclosure on the large lower deck. The day was chilly and we were grateful for some protection from the wind.

As long as I live, I'll never get used to the majestic mountains ringing town and lake. Lake Tranquility itself is large, over 2,000 acres in size. Two large islands and one small one gives the lake a racecourse footprint, yet the lake itself is large enough that you need a map to see it. The peaks surrounding it are stunning, an ever-changing panorama. I could see Mom's appreciation as well.

"I had no idea," she said with a smile. I love her face when it goes soft, when her thoughts are unprotected and wonder lights her eyes. "I see why you choose to live here."

We hadn't gone far when Mr. Ruskin joined us. "Mom, this is Leonard Ruskin, an art expert. This is my mother, Anna," I introduced. I'm sure Mr. Ruskin had an official occupational title, but I didn't know it. There wasn't a chance in hell he didn't recognize Mom, but I wasn't opening the door to that discussion by announcing her full name.

"Pleased to meet you," he said.

"What brings you to Tranquility?" Mom asked, shifting the focus to him right off the bat.

"I've worked with the painter Michael Michel for a number of years. I also have a few clients such as Mr. Cavalleros, whom I advise on their collections, and help them make informed decisions about sales and purchases."

In his current outfit, his hair made obedient by some sort of gel, he looked as if he'd be at home on a yacht.

"Where are you usually based?"

"Maryland. I lecture at Towson."

"How long have you been coming up here?"

He shook his head. "Twelve years? Fifteen?"

"Then I wonder," she said, sitting forward, her voice suddenly low and intense, "if you've heard the rumors about the missing treasure?"

"The Clarkson Collection?" he asked, eyebrows raised.

"The missing paintings by women artists."

"That's it!" he said, obviously enjoying this turn in the conversation. What have you heard?"

"Works by Mary Cassatt, Elizabeth Nourse."

"Berthe Morisot. Abigail May. To start the list."

"You must be intrigued."

"Who wouldn't be?"

"I'm sorry but what are you talking about?" I asked, thinking, here we go again, Mom somehow knows the thing, the *exact* subject to make anyone excited to converse with her. How on God's green earth would she know about the Clarkson Collection, when I lived here and I'd never heard of it?

Mom smiled at Leonard, passing the conversational baton to him—which he happily accepted. "I'm sure you know that in the 1800s and early 20TH century, the neighboring town of Saranac Lake was a haven for those suffering from tuberculosis. There was a sanitorium there, and many 'cure cottages' where people could come to breathe the clear mountain air."

"Even Robert Louis Stevenson came in search of relief from his symptoms," nodded Mom.

"As did an avid art collector named Dora Clarkson. She was an educated heiress, ahead of her time, who saw and appreciated the talent of emerging female painters. She collected as many of their works as she could. Her husband didn't understand her passion. Dora contracted tuberculosis and came up here to recuperate. She was afraid while she was gone that her husband would sell off her collection for a pittance, so she had the best paintings by now very well-known female artists packed up and shipped up with her. When Dora died, the paintings vanished. Simply vanished. Her heirs, friends, and even museum curators, came up to search for them. By the time of her death, the artworks were not only important, several of them displayed significant steps in the artistic journeys of the women who painted them."

"Never found?" I asked.

"Never," said Mom and Leonard together.

"Have you ever been tempted to look?" Mom queried.

"Well, I'm not enough of an outdoorsman to plan a search over any kind of radius. But I will admit I never pass a mountain cave without a look-see."

"How could you possibly hide paintings in a cave without ruining them?" I asked.

Leonard took the question seriously. "You've got a couple of options. You could have a local locksmith hide a good-sized safe inside. Or, the paintings could themselves have traveled in a tightly sealed, moisture-proof case of some sort."

"In any case, it seems the final job of hiding the works would require help. One sickly woman could hardly haul multiple paintings, let alone a safe, to a cave," Mom mused.

"That does seem likely. However, if she had help, no one ever came forward."

There was a slight jolt as the motors slowed in preparation for sliding into the Cavalleros' enclosed boathouse. We stayed put as the captain expertly steered into the boat's intended berth. His assistant jumped to the dock with the rope to pull us in. The three of us sat safely until the craft stopped moving.

"See you ladies inside," Ruskin said, rejoining our host who'd been with the captain.

As we collected our things, I asked, "How do you know the story of the lost Clarkson Collection?"

"The woman I was talking to—Jules Eckhardt. Don't spread it around, but she's more than just an art history professor at John Jay. She's also an expert on art theft and recovery. She's long been fascinated by the story of the lost paintings of Dora Clarkson."

"Ah. Is that what she's doing here?" I asked.

"Actually, no," she said. She'd lowered her voice to a whisper and put a hand on my arm. "She's here working with the state police. They're getting close to cracking a major ring of art thieves. These guys are pros. They've been at it for decades. Billions of dollars of art has passed through their hands."

"Did you say *billions*?"

She nodded.

"They sound dangerous."

"Very."

My mind whirred. Dangerous enough that someone would send a bounty hunter? And an assassin to kill a bounty hunter?

"Gee, I wonder if mild mannered Mr. Ruskin knows anything about it," I whispered. I was once again glad to get Mom away from the craziness back in town.

"All ashore!" called the captain.

"Possibly without even knowing it. Jules Eckhardt thinks Ruskin may be able to lead us to the mastermind," said Mom as we headed for the hulking man, Planton's steward, who offered a hand to help us from boat to dock.

THE LOST ART

Ingredients

> Chilled Champagne
> Frozen green grapes
> 1 oz elderflower liqueur
> Fresh lemon peel
> Fresh basil leaves
> Champagne glass

Method

Add frozen grapes and torn basil leaves to bottom of Champagne glass. Add elderflower liqueur and fill the rest of the glass with Champagne. Squeeze lemon peel and wipe around rim of glass. Drop lemon peel in cocktail.

9

UNMOORED

Normal parents would wear an awed expression upon entering a mansion such as the one the Cavalleros family uses as their summer getaway. However, my mother has visited every type of abode from hut to castle. She takes everything in stride—but also knows how to express the enthusiasm expected by billionaires. They at least want to see the reaction they've become oh-so-bored by.

The main floor of the Cavalleros mansion has ceilings that soar four stories tall. Arriving through the front door, you are magnetically pulled toward the massive back wall of windows which, in warmer weather, fold back completely to merge the house with the outdoor terraces and the lake. Most guests stand, drink somehow magically appearing in their hands, staring at the mesmerizing gentle waves of the lake beneath the jutting majesty of the mountains. The beckoning terraces are large enough to seat an entire symphony orchestra. I should know; I've dispensed drinks only feet from one.

But the lake was not the main draw for these particular guests. Midway through the room, a giant, modern chandelier draws the eye up a circular staircase to the second floor which is also two stories high. Lining these wall surfaces are the beginnings of Planton's art collection. This afternoon, no one made it past the staircase. Instead, Leonard Ruskin and Anna Nash stood, necks craned, eyes large, mouths slack, taking in the magnificent paintings before and above them.

The canvases themselves were huge. They had to be, to not get lost swimming in a wall of white. I'd noticed, when I'd been bumped

69

up from bartender to friend and thus welcomed to higher floors, that the art was abstract on the lower floors and leaned toward realism as you rose.

"Cecily Brown," Mom muttered, referring to the painter of a piece ten feet by nine feet at the least. It was a cyclone of color; reds, blues, yellows, in small specific, masterful strokes. "But... this one, too?"

Planton nodded. The one to which Mom was now referring was comparatively calming; yellows and greens, wed in rectangles.

"Striking," she said. "Both. My."

"I love how you're displaying the Bridget Riley," said Leonard, of a piece that featured an intriguing blend of lines and colors. They stood for a moment, musing on the specifics of the paintings.

That was fine with me. It was beginning to dawn on me that, by running away from the action and stranding myself here, I was truly trapped with Mom and whatever important discussion she wanted to have.

Damn.

"Wait. Is that—a Gerhard Richter?" Mom asked of a gigantic painting, maybe thirty feet by ten. The colors danced and swirled from left to right, deep blues, reds and yellows, bound together in a perfect invitation to movement toward a sphere that could be the sun.

"It is."

"I almost didn't recognize it. I haven't seen many of his abstracts. I'm so used to his detailed intersections of line and color."

"This one is stunning," said Leonard, referring to the next painting along the wall.

"It is," said Mom.

The work itself had reaches of color, some entwined, others screeching to a halt mid-painting.

Finally, Mr. Ruskin admitted, "I don't recognize the painter."

"Philip Young. Studied art alongside my son in Paris."

"Amazing," said the art expert. "But if you are collecting him, I'd expect nothing less."

I hid my smile. Neither Planton or I mentioned that the same Philip Young was the young man who'd invited my mother and me to this hideaway.

"My office is this way," announced Planton with a sweep of his hand, pointing Mr. Ruskin to the hallway behind the family breakfast room that housed his spacious professional suite. Then, to Mom, "Inez has been alerted and will prepare your rooms. Arturo will deliver your bag."

I assumed Arturo was the steward. I'd noticed him around, carefully melting into the background, during other visits. It made sense for Planton to have security besides his museum-quality alarm system, especially when he was here by himself off-season. Arturo – bald, dressed in black trousers and a white shirt—remained outside Planton's office. He wore an earpiece.

As if by magic, Inez, the housekeeper, appeared, a very tall willowy woman wearing a mix of reds and oranges, colors I thought of as inherently Spanish. She said, "I'll be back when the room is made up. And I'm sure you could use something to eat?"

"Thank you."

Inez skirted away, speaking briefly to Arturo, who went to deliver Mom's bag to her quarters. This left Mom and me now standing, looking toward the lake and the November skies beyond.

"Shall we sit?" she asked.

Modular sofas ran the length of the room in slightly different shades, each hue fashioned into conversation squares. We chose a center sofa, its cushions a soft yellow. Although it was just us, we planted ourselves in a corner, Mom facing the lake, me close by on the side. It was odd to be alone in a space meant for multitudes.

We sat for a few minutes, catching our breath.

I was used to this. At home, Mom is quiet. She's a natural introvert. On days when she's not working, she wears no make-up and lets her hair drip-dry. For all her listening skills with everyone else in the world, when we had been alone in my youth, I often felt she was somewhere else. She'd usually hear what I had to say, but only after shaking her head as if to rejoin me, saying, "What was that again?"

Some of Mom's friends have nicknames for their celebrity alter-egos. They aren't usually quite as dramatic as, say, Sasha Fierce, but there is a distinction between the private person and the public persona. I wouldn't say Mom switches personalities as much as she flips an *on* switch. When I was a kid, I wished there was a middle ground.

Her partner, Kali Sanborn, is an environmental lawyer. Tall, fair-skinned, hair below her shoulders and dark, dark brown, it's as if Kali wakes up already put together. As one might expect, at home Kali speaks faster and more loudly. She knows what has to get done and was usually at it, slaying dragons either in person or over the phone.

She was also good at giving Mom a wink or a secret smile to signal she was grounded, even in the middle of a legal battle.

You might see how, with all this going on, I chose to drop out of college to become a bartender.

"I love your pub," Mom said. "It's what I would invent in my head if I was trying to describe the perfect meeting place."

"Thanks."

She sat forward with curiosity. "What is going on with the gingerbread contest? It seems in a bit of disarray."

"To say the least."

"Why don't they just postpone it?"

"I don't think they can. They'd have to cancel it and try again next year."

"That might work better."

"It turns out Stormie Edwards, the head sous chef for Pepper's restaurant, is dating the producer. It's his first full producing credit at the network so there's a lot riding on it. I like Stormie. I hope it works out for them. Though it is seeming less and less likely."

We sat silently again, gathering our thoughts. I did want to know what was so important Mom felt she had to see me in person to discuss it—though I knew I probably didn't want to discuss it.

"I think you impressed them with your knowledge of living artists," I said.

"I figured if I was going to get any information at all for Professor Eckhardt, I'd best position myself to be part of the club."

And... that's all it took.

Here, I'd gone to all the trouble to get Mom out of the danger zone, across a lake to an inaccessible house. I'd even tagged Marta in for the night and taken off from my shift when things were going bonkers at MacTavish's—to be here, to keep her as safe as I could. And the first thing she did was purposefully prove her worthiness for the Art Theft Art League, currently set upon by dangerous predators?

"What the fuck, mom! Didn't you just tell me Professor Eckhardt was working with authorities to bring down a very dangerous ring of criminals? Hasn't there just been a hit on a bounty hunter at the hotel where you're staying? Wasn't there a naked rapist in your room?"

Oh, dear God. Was I the only one who could go from zero to 120 in high-speed fury at the much-beloved Anna Nash?

She looked at me, remaining calm as usual. As annoyingly usual.

"We came all this way for you to be safe," I repeated urgently but quietly, trying to keep our conversation private.

"I do understand. And thank you for that. I want you to know that I do take threatening situations seriously. If we know I'm being stalked, or the safety of my room has been breached, I have no interest in pressing my luck. I will for sure play it safe."

"You always say that," was my best answer.

"You don't need to be scared of losing me," she said. It seemed an outlandish thing to say, given that we weren't together these days at all. But I knew it was exactly the point. My father had up and left. My best friend had died of an overdose. I myself had come close enough to death to understand in my bones that it was a real thing, something you couldn't control. A situation that allows no do-overs.

I hated how much I needed her. How much I had to share her with others—with the world. How lost I'd be without her.

"What were you needing to talk about?" I didn't want to enter the discussion as much as I wanted to get it over with.
She paused, switching gears.

"Wait. You and Kali aren't breaking up, are you?"

"No, no, nothing like that. Me and your aunts and uncles are trying to settle Mormor's and Morfar's estate. It's complicated and, frankly, soul-sucking. The hardest part is watching items that belonged to them, that were so precious to them, lose their meaning and become just... things."

"Soul-sucking," I sympathized

"Here's what I want to talk to you about. The Engstrom brownstone. It's been in the family for one hundred years now, purchased for your great grandparents in Brooklyn as a wedding gift from your great-great-grandfather."

"Next door to the Bentons," I added, referencing the Black family who'd become their best friends for many decades. The grandchildren, including myself and Reggie Benton, the cousin nearest my age, spent summers at the Brooklyn brownstone. I remembered us going with Mormor to the local farmer's market early on summer mornings before the heat set in; playing hide and seek with Reggie at the Botanical Gardens; poring over photo albums of relatives spanning generations. I was headed for that very brownstone—and I was almost there—when I got off the cross-country train from California to make my final connection into New York. If it hadn't been for the family brownstone, I would never have been in Tranquility to have lunch at the Battened Hatch, which started my new life. Which started everything.

"Yes. What about the brownstone?"

"We need to figure out what to do with it. It is not only full of memories and family history, it's worth a lot of money. The thing is, of us five kids, no one wants to sell it, but no one wants to live there, either. Your aunts and uncles figure I'm the only one with the money to buy it. They want me to keep the place and buy them out. That way they get the money as their inheritance and they can visit the place for holidays, or whenever they want to."

"What? They want you to live there?"

"Or they want me to buy it for you. The bottom line is, they don't care who lives there. They want to have their money and access to the brownstone, too."

"Oh." This was a lot to take in. The truth was, it was hard for me to imagine the brownstone gone, belonging to strangers. And yet it certainly wasn't in my plans to move to Brooklyn, New York.

"So, what…? I mean, do you actually have enough money to buy the brownstone?"

"Not without a lot of maneuvering. More to the point, not to buy it as a keepsake."

"Would it be a sound investment? To rent it out, I mean?"

"Your mormor wasn't well for a while. There are a lot of upkeep things that need to happen, like a new furnace, new windows—big ticket items like that. And I have little interest in becoming a land-lord."

I had no interest in becoming one, either. But the idea of losing a place that meant home and family to me brought a sharp physical pain.

"Life moves on. I frankly don't know anyone else who still lives in a homestead that's been in their family for over a hundred years. I wanted to make sure you weren't dying to move to New York City."

"Not right now. But it feels sad to know that if I do someday, the brownstone will be gone."

"I know."

"Will your siblings be mad at you?"

"I wouldn't be surprised."

"But… why should it be up to you to save the house and give them money?"

"Who doesn't want to have their cake and eat it, too? I mean, if it's an option."

I leaned backwards into the cushions. Was I thinking of the brownstone—of Brooklyn—in an idealized way? When I pictured it, Mormor was there, my cousins were there, everything was clean and smelling of cinnamon and cardamom and baking bread. I don't bake bread. I knew my memories of it were leaning into hiraeth territory.

"What are you thinking?" Mom asked.

"I'm thinking it makes me feel a bit unmoored."

"That's a good word for it. Which is what makes it hard to bring up the next topic. Kali and I are thinking of selling the house."

"The California house? Our house?"

"Yes. With you gone, we don't really need that much square footage. Not to mention coastal Southern California doesn't seem the best place to settle long-term, what with the fires and floods and landslides and earthquakes and insurance companies pulling out right and left."

Was she kidding me?

Already off balance from the loss of the ancestral home, this pushed me fully off the cliff.

I couldn't speak. I didn't know until that moment how much I loved our house. It was full of windows and bright sunshine, and I thought of it as a hobbit-hole in the best possible way, a place of safety from the stupid, plastic world of Los Angeles all around me. It was where my friends gathered after school if we weren't headed for Salty Sally's.

It was the launching pad that sent me out into the world, and, if need be, gave me a landing spot on return.

I was losing both of my landing spots at once. Mom was settled. She had Kali. She could move on to new frontiers and take her home with her. She and Kali were each other's home.

I had nothing. As much as I loved my rented cottage, it was a rental, transient by definition.

It had been a long time since I'd had a panic attack, but I was headed for one now.

Not wanting to go there, not wanting to show my mother how affected I was by her announcement, I said, "I've got to go get my friend's jacket before I forget."

And I bolted from the room.

As I did, I heard Planton's office door open and he and Ruskin step out.

"Thanks for showing me your black book," said Planton.

"And perhaps, someday, the red book."

"Someday, perhaps."

"It takes a little more guts to shop from the red book."

"If that's what you want to call it."

Obviously, the men thought they were alone and unheard. They weren't.

"I'd be interested to see the book," came a new voice. My mother's.

I looked back to see her standing casually on the few stairs which led up from the seating area.

The men looked her way, surprised.

"Black or red, you choose. I'm in an artsy mood." Her smile was infectious.

She was, after all, Anna Nash.

UNMOORED

Ingredients

1 ½ Hendricks Gin
4 fresh carrots
¼ teaspoon sea salt
¼ tsp fresh ground black pepper
1 fresh lemon cut into quarters
Fresh cherry heirloom tomatoes for garnish
Fresh heirloom tomatoes for juicing (any variety, any size)
High ball glass
Crushed ice
Cocktail shaker

Method

Juice carrots and cherry heirloom tomatoes and pour 5 oz into cocktail shaker. Add ice, a pinch each of salt and pepper, and gin. Squeeze a quarter of fresh lemon into shaker and shake vigorously until ingredients are blended. Place the rest of salt and pepper on a small plate and mix together.
Rub a wedge of lemon around rim of high ball glass and dip rim of glass onto plate with salt and pepper.
Pour contents of cocktail shaker into rimmed glass and add a piece of carrot stem and heirloom cherry tomato for garnish.

10
RED ALERT

FORTUNATELY, I KNEW where the elevator was.

The lower two floors were for entertaining and business. The third floor was for guests who were staying over, the fourth for the two grown Cavalleros offspring when they were in residence. The top floor was the primary quarters for Planton and Alise. I'd never seen it.

I had, however, spent happy hours in the suite of rooms belonging to Tomás, watching movies and eating pizza with him and Philip. It was there I was likely to find Philip's coat. I got off on four. Only then did it occur to me to wonder if the currently-uninhabited rooms would be locked. I wasn't eager to explain to Inez or, God forbid, Arturo, why I needed the key.

Thankfully, the door slid open.

I hit the light switch and chose my illumination level. Tomás' private living room sprang to life around me. I went to the tall closet on the far wall and found exactly what I was looking for: one black faux-leather coat. I took it off the hanger and wandered back into the room, where I fell into a cushioned chair, holding the coat to me tightly.

I wasn't used to having panic attacks and I didn't want to start getting used to it now. I drew deep breaths and decided not to even think about the possibility of my imminent homelessness.

About being adrift.

Instead, I hugged the coat and thought about art. About Philip, currently heading to the airport to leave me when I needed him most.

About Inspector Mike Spaulding bringing the art recovery woman into the pub, into my world, and introducing her to my mother.

About there being a dangerous ring of professional art thieves raking in billions. Billions with a b, surely enough to search or kill for.

Which led my thoughts from billions, to art, to crazy-expensive masterpieces, to Planton who was a billionaire with a b with masterpieces and a house protected with layers of security and a private office where he met with Leonard Ruskin who might, even inadvertently, meet with the mastermind.

Oh. Dear. God.

Was Planton an art-theft mastermind? Was he ruthless? Did he hire assassins?

Surely Philip wouldn't hang out with Tomás if his father was a thief. But maybe if he didn't know?

All I knew was, I would feel so much better if I heard Philip's voice.

There was no phone signal on this side of the lake, but my phone had jumped onto the Wi-Fi; I had entered the password on a previous visit. If someone turned it off, we'd have no communication with the rest of the world. I grabbed my phone and tapped Philip's name.

He didn't pick up. He was likely at the airport. If he was in line to go through security, he couldn't pick up.

Damn.

As long as I was online, I checked the weather app. The announcement at the top had turned an angry red: Tranquility had gone from being under a winter storm watch to being under a winter storm warning. A blizzard was on its way, hitting late tonight or early tomorrow morning. I was grateful I'd be back in town well before then.

Hugging Philip's coat for courage, I returned to the elevator and headed downstairs.

Mom was gone.

Planton came out of the kitchen, Inez trailing him carrying a tray with two crystal wine glasses and a carafe of red wine. He saw me standing there, alone and looking confused.

"Your mother has gone to her rooms," he said. "The Rose Guest Suite on the third floor, I believe."

I remembered the Birthday Bash I worked here, how Mr. Cavalleros came through and spoke appreciatively to each staff member. Now his demeanor was cold and businesslike. He was sturdy. Someone with whom you didn't mess. I'd never been afraid of him before. I hope it didn't show now.

He reentered his office. Inez delivered the wine and left, shutting the door behind her.

She turned to me. "Yes, the Rose Suite. The elevator is back this way."

"Thank you," I said. "I know where it is."

On the third floor, I was relieved to discover I hadn't stayed in the Rose Suite. It held no special memories for me.

The door was slightly ajar, but I knocked anyway.

"Come in, come in."

Mom stood in the middle of the living room, fiddling with her phone. A fire crackled in the fireplace—real logs, properly dried. An elaborate charcuterie board was set out on the table in front of the sofas, along with a wine decanter and a coffee pot.

"Do you know the Wi-Fi password?" she asked.

I gave it to her. Immediately her phone exploded with messages. She scrolled through them

"Nothing immediate," she said.

I didn't want to get back into discussing our homes. I didn't want to chide her again for stepping into dangerous waters.

Well, yes. Yes, I fucking did. Was she trying to get herself killed while visiting me, to make sure it was my fault?

"So what was in the black book and the red book?" I asked, thinking about the conversation I'd overheard.

She sat down and poured us each a glass of Rioja. Then she looked around the room, as if seeing it for the first time. "This is a crazy mansion."

"Indeed it is."

"The books are catalogues of art pieces for sale. I didn't get to look at them long because Mr. Ruskin had not yet run my credit score and bank accounts to make sure I was really in the market. But he suspects I might clear the bar, so he let me peruse. Nothing costs less than several mill. The Black Book presents pieces of art with clean lines of ownership—i.e. they're legal to sell and own. He was much more reticent about letting me see the Red Book. It's got some pretty amazing pieces. Well, they both do. But my understanding is that, since the pieces in the Red Book may have been on the black market at some time, their lines of ownership aren't completely traceable. He claims they actually are, and that his firm is in the business of cleaning it all up, but for those willing to purchase before all the work is done and before it goes to auction, the prices will be much better."

"That sounds fishy."

"Or pretty interesting. I honestly don't know enough about art's black market—or even its 'grey' one—to know if this is mighty suspicious or par for the course with private collections."

"Did you give him your banking info?"

"Was I born yesterday? No. Since my time with the books was so limited, we agreed we'd talk back in town."

She held up her glass. "The wine's good. Rioja is Spanish, of course. I'll have to inquire which one this is."

It was growing dark outside, which begged the question: Did I feel right about leaving Mom here by herself with Planton and Arturo? If Planton was somehow involved in the art ring, and if I were Planton, I might be concerned she was getting too clued in about finding out too much about my art involvement.

All he'd need to do would be to turn off the Internet router and she'd be cut off from contact with me, or the police for that matter.

"I want to see the bedroom," she said. "Come on."

I already knew how cool the bedrooms were, with comfy sitting areas, and bathrooms the size of Monaco, floors and towel racks all heated.

As Mom stood up, her phone rang. It startled both of us. Who gets in touch by phone call anymore? She looked at the device in her hand for several seconds.

"Who is it?" I asked.

"I don't know. It's a local number." She considered a minute longer, then accepted the call. "Hello."

Her posture relaxed. "Okay, thanks for letting me know. I appreciate it. I accept. I'll let you know when I'll be there."

She ended the call and gave a crooked smile. "They caught the guy who was waiting in my room."

"That's good news."

"And MacTavish's has moved me to a suite with a private hall that they can protect more easily."

Ah, I knew the suite. It had been Pepper Porter's living quarters, back in the day.

"What do you think? Should I spend the night, as long as I'm here?"

I went to the window and gazed out, wondering when my ride with Leonard Ruskin and the boat captain would be heading back. Maybe I should start downstairs, as darkness was gathering quickly.

I looked toward the boathouse, which was hung with lights, expecting to see the boat similarly illuminated. I didn't see it. Maybe it was just too dark, or the boat had run errands and had berthed in a different slip I couldn't see?

No. It wasn't there. I let my eyes adjust and scanned farther out. The boat had pushed off from the Cavalleros dock and was already on the water, turned and headed back for the far shore. It was maybe thirty feet gone. I could make out the form of Leonard Ruskin.

Was that the plan all along? To bring us here and strand us?

I looked at my phone.

The little Wi-Fi symbol was gone.

A blizzard was heading this way. No one would have any way to know where we were or if we were in serious trouble for at least a couple of days, or longer if the storm made the lake impassable. Until then, we were at the mercy of Planton and his very large caretaker.

RED ALERT

Ingredients

Cocktail

2 oz rosé wine
1 ½ oz Pama liqueur
2 oz pomegranate juice
Ice
Cocktail shaker
Rocks glass

Black lemon foam

3 oz lemon juice
2 oz simple syrup
4 egg whites
Whipped cream dispenser
2 N2O chargers
1 activated charcoal capsule

Method

Black lemon foam
In whipped cream dispenser, add egg whites, lemon juice, simple syrup, and 1 activated charcoal capsule (break open and pour into dispenser). Put the top of the dispenser on and shake until all ingredients are blended. Add 2 N2O chargers to the container.
Store in refrigerator when not using. Shake every time before use.
Cocktail
In cocktail shaker, add ice, Pama liqueur, pomegranate

juice, and rosé. Shake together and pour into rocks glass. To finish cocktail, add a dollop of black lemon foam to the top.

11

SCENARIOS

"Grab your bag," I said to Mom. "The only boat is heading for shore. And we've got to be on it."

She heard the urgency in my voice.

"Where is it?" she asked. Her bag, a supple black carry-all, was nowhere to be seen.

She scanned the room while I opened the guest closet. Mom's bag was there, sitting on a luggage rack. It was empty.

"Avalon, what's going on?"

"Trust me, Mom, we've got to be on that boat. It might not be safe here."

She joined me in front of the closet, where Inez had hung many of her clothes. She pulled them down and stuffed them into the bag. Then she opened the top drawer of the dresser, also in the closet. Her undergarments were there. She grabbed them too.

"Anything missing? In the bathroom?" I asked.

"I'll go look."

"I'm going to run down to the dock and try to bring back the boat. Once you've got your stuff, head to the stairway. It's at the end of the hall just to the right. Don't wait for the elevator." *Or risk being stuck in it if someone turns off the power.*

"Avalon..."

"I know. I'm sorry. I have to run if I have any hope of catching the boat."

She headed for the bathroom and I tore through the living room, out into the hall, and through the door at the end which led to the private staircase.

As fast as I'd been running, my cast had rubbed my skin off in patches around the top. I stood at the top of the stairs and panted. Since each of the bottom two floors were two stories high, I would have to hobble down four flights of stairs. The boat would be gone.

As much as I didn't trust the elevator, it was my only hope. With luck, no one thought Mom and I suspected anything about the possibility of being virtual prisoners here. Fortunately, the elevator was waiting on the third floor. It took me down rapidly. I immediately sent it back up for Mom, just in case.

I took a deep breath, praying no one was around and race-walked (well, race-clunked) through the living room, out past the terrace and down to the dock.

Once there, my heart sank.

The boat was quite far away. My only hope was to make enough noise to catch their attention. If both Leonard and the captain were in on the plan to keep us here, we were sunk. But if one of them, either one, was not, there was a chance they'd turn around. "Leonard!" I yelled. "Leonard!"

There was nothing metallic to bang on, but I picked up an oar and waved it around, thunking it against the dock railings. I walked to the end of the dock so they'd know I was calling for them.

"Leonard!" a second voice joined in as Mom joined me on the dock. She picked up an orange life vest with reflective tape and waved it through the air.

It seemed as though we were too late.

Finally, Leonard Ruskin turned around and saw movement on the dock behind him. He craned forward, puzzled.

Having worked it out it was us, he went inside the boat's cabin and shut the door.

Mom and I looked at each other for a long moment. Was he gone?

Slowly, the boat began to circle back.

"Should I go back and say thanks to Planton Cavalleros?" Mom asked.

"No!"

She looked surprised but accepted the sentiment. "Okay. I did see Inez and told her something had come up."

I prayed the boat would arrive before Inez could tell Planton we were making a run for it.

The motor became louder as the boat approached, then slowed and pulled into the slip. The captain held it steady while Mom handed her bag to Leonard, then took his hand and stepped down into the boat.

I looked up the hill toward the house. Inez stood, watching us.

I sat down hard on the dock and slid into the boat cast-first.

As the boat reversed, Arturo exited the house and stood next to Inez. He put a hand to his ear and spoke a few words. Was he telling Planton we were making a getaway? Or arranging to have someone meet us once we reached the opposite shore?

Not till the boat had pulled back out and opened the throttle did I breathe a sigh of relief.

Following Mom's example, I turned and waved to Inez and Arturo, as if we were simply heading home after a pleasant stay.

Any warmth from the day had departed at sundown, so we all went inside the cabin.

"Didn't you guys promise I could ride back tonight?" I asked Leonard.

"Yes, I'm sorry, Inez said she thought you were staying. She'd been asked to put food in the guest quarters."

Okay, I can see how it could have been an innocent mistake on Inez's part. After all, only Leonard and Planton were privy to the discussion at MacTavish's that had me coming back tonight.

"I was a little concerned about leaving you with the blizzard coming and all." Leonard said.

Mom thanked him and reported that they'd caught the intruder back at the hotel, and she needed to return for a work commitment—especially with the threat of snow.

"Do you have a car waiting?" I asked the art expert.

"No, I was going to call a cab."

"I have a guy," I said. "Are you heading for MacTavish's?"

"Yes. I'd like to share a ride if you get one. Thanks."

I texted Jeff, who was indeed available to head for the wharf. As I sent our exact docking location, I got a new text, this one from Philip.

At the airport. Just realized I don't have the keys to my Paris apartment. Is there a chance you could pick them up at my place and have Jeff bring them to the airport?

I'll do my best, I answered.

I'll wait outside security if he can come.

He told me where in his house to look.

I admit I was nervous as we approached the dock. Worst case scenario, Leonard Ruskin and the boat captain both worked for Planton and we'd be hustled into a black SUV and taken to an undisclosed location.

Best case scenario, Leonard Ruskin was an art professor, the boat captain piloted Planton's boats when needed, Mom and I would arrive safely back at MacTavish's.

In neither scenario was Noel Schlessinger alive. And neither left me with a home.

SCENARIOS

Ingredients

This is a batch recipe
1 bottle red wine (your choice)
4 oz brandy
1 fresh orange
6 cinnamon sticks
¼ teaspoon mulling spices
1 teaspoon raw sugar
1 medium saucepan
Cocktail mugs (makes 4 servings)

Method

Add wine, brandy, 2 cinnamon sticks, mulling spices, raw sugar, and a few slices of fresh oranges to a medium saucepan. Steep over medium heat for about 20 minutes on low heat, stirring occasionally. Ladle warm mulled wine into cocktail mug and finish with fresh orange slices and 1 cinnamon stick each.

12

LADDER OUT OF HELL

JEFF'S CAB WAITED on the shore. It took him, Leonard, and my mom to help me clamber onto the dock. I was ready to get a hatchet and remove the cast myself.

As Mom and Leonard loaded themselves into the car, I chatted with Jeff outside, asking if he could run Philip's keys to the airport. He said the night was slow as everyone had heard the storm warning and were battening their hatches. He could help out.

Mom and Leonard gave their okay for me to pick up keys for a friend on our way to the hotel.

Philip's craftsman-style house was on a short, level street off a steep road. The porch light was on. "I'll be right back," I said to the folks in the car. I had the key to the side door. A motion sensor light sprang on as I climbed the wooden stairs. I entered the alarm code, then unlocked the door itself. I pushed into the small hallway and turned left toward the living quarters rather than right toward Philip's large studio.

The house was chilly as he had the thermostat turned down. I went through the kitchen and living room, turning on lights as I went. Then I went into his bedroom. I turned on the overhead light as well as the lamp on the bedside by the closet.

He said the set of keys was in his closet in a sock.

That's correct, in a sock.

Somehow, I expected there to be a sock sitting on top of his dresser. There was none.

I opened the second drawer down, which was his sock drawer. Surely there would be a mateless sock, hibernating in a corner?

None that I could see. Many of his socks had moved to my place, but he still had a nice selection here: thick white workout socks to the left, darker dress socks to the right. I began feeling the toes of every darned sock.

Exasperated, I called him, hit speaker, and put the phone on top of the dresser while I continued sorting through the socks.

"Hey," he answered. "Thanks so much. Did you get them?"

"I'm in your bedroom closet," I said. "You apparently have them very well hidden. Do you truly think some crook who wants to go to Paris, would think, 'I know, I'll break into Philip's house and rifle through his socks in case there's a key to an unidentified apartment?'"

He chuckled. "It should be on top of the dresser."

"No go, Joe. Should I send you a photo?"

"No need. Hmm. Maybe it fell on the floor?"

Great. It's not as easy to get down on the floor with a cast on as one might hope. But once down, I crawled, reaching through shadows, feeling the empty floor.

"By the way, Mom came back with me from the Cavalleros' house. They caught her hotel stalker."

"That's good, I guess."

"Say, what do you know about what Planton does for work?"

"Only what I've seen online. Why?"

"Nothing illegal, as far as you know?"

"No. Why are you asking?"

"Apparently, there's a billion-dollar art theft ring. He has art and, well, billions."

"Oooh, gentleman robber?"

"That's the TV version, I guess. You don't know anything?"

"I do not. But if he was involved, it would be high-stakes. He's that kind of guy."

My cast was chafing and I was becoming more annoyed. As a last resort, I felt my way around the dresser and reached behind it.

And there was a big lumpy sock. I pulled it out and emptied

the set of keys into my hand. Then I crawled to the bed and hauled myself up and went back for the phone.

"You owe me," I said.

"More than I can ever repay," he said.

"Jeff will drop us at MacTavish's and head your way."

"Au revoir."

"Bye."

I reversed my route, turning off lights as I went. Once in the living room, I heard sounds coming from the kitchen. Confused, I slid to the side of the door and peeked through. It was Jeff, at the sink, filling his water bottle.

"Thought I might as well get a drink and use the john," he said. "No point in waiting in the car by myself. Hope you don't mind."

"No, of course not, it's fine. But—in the car by yourself? Where are my mom and Mr. Ruskin?"

Jeff tilled his head back toward Philip's studio. Light spilled through the door which now sat halfway open.

Oh, holy heck.

I went to the stairs which led down to the studio.

Mom and Leonard had turned on all the lights, including the spotlights, against the gathering darkness outside. The tall white walls glistened, but the woods beyond the yawning windows were lost.

Philip taught painting to some local students, including Marta, who was quite talented. His students' work was in an alcove. The rest of the work throughout the room was his own.

Philip had recently gone through a hard time, had plunged into a dark space in which he couldn't deal with the world. His release was making art. This hadn't resulted in a nice canvas tucked here and another leaning there; the room was an explosion of art, of color, of movement, of fear and longing, of fury and betrayal, of love and misunderstanding. These paintings were the ladder he'd built to climb out of hell.

Many of the canvases were 36 by 48. Many were larger. Several were ten feet tall at least.

Neither Mom nor Leonard looked up as I entered. I stayed at the top of the wide white steps which curtsied down into the space.

"Excuse me," I said.

It was as if I wasn't there.

"Excuse me?" A little louder. Nothing.

"Mom? Leonard?" I shouted.

They each stopped what they were doing and looked up.

"We need to go. Now."

"Can you come back for me?" Leonard asked.

"No. Now."

Chastened, but not very, they both reluctantly headed toward me. Each of them stopped three or four more times, just to take in the enormity of a painting. At one point, Leonard took out his phone to take a photo.

"No," I said, surprised at the sound of my own authority. "You can see anything he feels is ready for public consumption on his website."

Leonard walked past me first. Jeff was in the back hallway and held the outside door open as they exited.

As Mom walked past me, she whispered, "Holy shit. You know this person?"

"Yes. I do."

I turned off all the studio lights, and those in the back hall, as well. Then I locked the door and reset the alarm.

As I handed the keys to Jeff, I felt nauseous. Had I just led a top-tier art thief to Philip's collection?

LADDER OUT OF HELL

Ingredients

1 oz dark rum
1 oz blue curaçao liqueur
4 oz whole milk
Fresh orange peel
1 Luxardo cherry
Pinch of fresh ground cinnamon
Ice
Cocktail shaker
Rocks glass

Method

Chill a rocks glass in freezer beforehand.
Fill chilled glass halfway with ice cubes. Slowly pour dark rum over the ice to start building layers, rum will fall to bottom due to its higher density. Then gently pour the blue curaçao over the back of the spoon held just above the rum layer to create a distinct blue layer. Finally, pour the milk over the back of a different spoon to create a top layer, this should float on top due to its lower density.
Add a pinch of cinnamon, fresh orange peel and Luxardo cherry for garnish.
To drink, slowly stir all ingredients together to combine drink after presenting.

13
BATTENING THE HATCHES

IT WAS NINE-THIRTY p.m. when we returned and MacTavish's was bustling. Leonard Ruskin peeled off and went in through the main lobby entrance. I took Mom in through the Battened Hatch's street door. Only then did I feel I'd safely returned to my home turf. The pub was fairly empty. Folks did indeed seem to heading for shelter, battening their own hatches against the approaching storm.

I guided Mom to the end of the bar, to a seat by itself in the shadows, and went out to find security. Fortunately, Nelson was still on. I told him Anna Karenina was back. He went to get a key to suite seven. He asked me to give him a minute and then bring Anna and meet him there. I knew well where it was.

Marta and Mom were chatting at the bar as I returned. "Can we close early?" Marta asked. "I've got to get to the set to help Emelia."

"The shoot is still on?" I asked.

"Seems that way. Darla West, the host from the Delicious Food Network, has arrived after all. The producer is in New York and there's going to be a hookup in an hour so he can check in with cast and crew."

"Yes, we can close. Things here are obviously slowing down. Manuela can close out the final checks. And yes, you can go to the set—but can I borrow you for a minute first, please?"

"What? Why? I mean, sure."

"Don't tell anybody, but they're moving Mom to suite seven. I just want you to... okay it."

She smiled. "I can do that."

Preparations were quickly made for closing; Manuela was on top of things and eager to head home herself.

Marta, Mom, and I exited through the lobby door and walked quickly, heads down, across and into a far hall. Two turns and we entered the private corridor leading to suite seven. Nelson already had a security guy at the hall entrance. He nodded at us.

"This is the suite where Pepper Porter stayed when she was in residence," I said quietly.

"Sounds nice."

Nelson opened the door. Lights were on in the living room and in the bedroom. Tall curtains were closed, blocking the lake view, except for one by the door that opened to the terraces overlooking the lake. The terraces were private and hard to see from elsewhere unless you were having a party with lights and music. Inside, the suite was 3,000 square feet, easy. It had recently been redone after a fire. It was elegant in an art deco décor that was at odds with the rest of the inn but true to the original design; it was lovely and bright. One black-and-white photo of Pepper Porter, smiling, sitting on the sofa in this room, sat framed on a side table.

"I've checked it out. Everything's in order," Nelson said. He handed Mom the key.

"Thank you, I appreciate it," she said. And with that, he was gone.

Marta wandered into the bedroom, while Mom and I found the Champagne bucket on the living room table. "This will be nice for later," Mom said.

"Want to see the view of the lake? It's really pretty."

Together, we walked out into the chilly night air. A just-past-full moon was hidden behind quickly moving clouds, but it gave enough light to show the fairyland of the inn reflected in the lake before us.

A marble balustrade ran the length of the marble terrace, which stretched from bedroom along the living room. The outdoor furniture had been moved to the far end, tucked against the outside wall, and covered for the winter.

"So, why did we have to get back tonight? I'm glad we did, as I don't want to be stranded across the lake if there's a blizzard, but it seemed you felt strongly about that one boat."

"You yourself said Ruskin might lead us to the ringleader, knowingly or not. I'm sure Planton Cavalleros is a fine fellow. I like his son. But leaving you there alone when you know there's a black book and a red book, didn't feel safe. And then the Wi-Fi went out. You'd have been really stuck there, not able to communicate with the outside world, for God knows how long."

"And that Arturo guy," Mom said. "Was he straight from central casting, or what?"

We laughed.

"In any case," she said, "I'm here to see you. I would have gone nuts there without phone or text. There's a lot going on. Professor Eckhardt may be well acquainted with Leonard's books of available art. If not, she might find them quite interesting."

"I have no doubt," I said. "You're not going to give him enough personal information that he'll show them to you again?"

"I don't know how else to do it. I've already texted Jules but I haven't heard back. I'd like her take on all this."

"And I thought academia was boring," I said.

"We're good," said Marta, sticking her head out through the sliding glass door.

We turned and headed for warmth as Mom asked, "If you don't mind my asking, what are we good with?"

Marta looked at me, silently asking me to give an appropriate answer.

"Marta is a sensitive," I said. "She can see dead people. Anyway, for years, Pepper Porter had left suite seven, but she hadn't quite moved on."

"She had a final piece of business," Marta said.

"You get more interesting every time you open your mouth," Anna said.

Marta actually blushed. "In any case, she's not here now. Her business was finished. Nothing but positive energy."

"Good to know."

Marta's phone dinged, and mine vibrated in my pocket as well.

"It's Emelia. I've got to go," said Marta.

Mine was, surprisingly, from Sous Chef Stormie. *All hell is breaking loose. Is there a chance you can come hold my hand for a minute?*

"I'm going to head for the set, too," I said.

"Well, I'm not sitting around here by myself," Mom said.

She dropped her bag in the bedroom and we all went out together.

BATTENING THE HATCHES

Ingredients

> 2 oz cognac or brandy of your choice
> 1 oz Cointreau (orange liqueur)
> ½ oz fresh lemon juice
> Raw sugar
> Fresh lemon peel for garnish
> Cocktail shaker
> Ice
> Rocks glass

Method

> Pour a small amount of raw sugar onto a small plate. Rub fresh lemon peel around the rim of the glass, then dip into raw sugar on plate.
> In cocktail shaker fill with ice, cognac or brandy, Cointreau, and fresh lemon juice. Shake ingredients until combined and chilled, then strain into cocktail glass. Finish by twisting fresh lemon peel over glass to release the citrus oil, use lemon peel as garnish.

14

HELL BREAKS LOOSE

THE SET WAS oddly quiet as we entered the adjoined confer-ence rooms. The eight bakers were at their stations, keeping to themselves.

Emelia was at a center workstation. Her supplies were neatly arrayed. She had a color printout of final baking and assembling instructions, which would culminate in a large pirate ship on a beach with a treasure chest. She even had the number of pieces of gingerbread and other edible supplies that would go into each sec-tion. Bakers were allowed two non-edible additions to their cre-ations. Hers would be a fabric sail and a small fan to blow wind into it.

As Marta joined Emelia behind the table, I looked around for Stormie.

It didn't take long to spot her. A confab was going on in the back end of the room. It involved Lucas, the main camera man, Darla the newly-arrived host, Will Acton the director, and Stormie the unof-ficial facilitator. Voices were raised. It answered the question of what spread a wet blanket over the rest of the room.

Marta stayed with Emelia while I headed toward Stormie and the gang.

"No, we can't break down and start again in a few hours. What are you, nuts? Union rules—everyone gets eight hours off between shifts!" The camera operator was getting all up in Will Acton's face. "You have no idea what you're doing, do ya, buddy?"

It's never good when the camera operator calls the director buddy.

"Look, it's my first solo directing gig. Gimme a break!"

"There's no time for a break! We're talking to New York in twenty!" screeched Darla. "How did this happen? Why did Tomie hire you? Why in God's name am I here?"

"I don't have to take this! I've never worked with such an outrageously ungrateful and unhelpful crew in my entire life!" Will Acton bellowed. With a dramatic flourish, he turned on his heel. We all watched in silence as the director stomped off and out of the room. In the cartoon version, there would have been smoke coming out of his ears.

The rest of us stood, staring.

"Should we go after him?" asked Esther Ringwald, the production coordinator.

"No!" answered everyone else at once.

A defeated silence prevailed.

"We talk to New York in twenty," said Darla. "I guess we pull the plug."

Across the room, someone laughed. They were joined by a second person.

Another baker gave a happy shout.

We turned as a group to find the world's most adorable Pomeranian being picked up by Marta. The dog licked Marta, then licked Emelia and looked adoringly at Gretl Haus who reached out to pet her.

It was Philip's dog, Whistle—safely ensconced at my cottage, last I knew.

The neurons in my brain could not bind together to find an explanation. Then in the midst of the suddenly-happy group of contestants, I saw Philip. Philip, who was supposed to be on a flight to Boston with keys to his Paris apartment in his pocket.

My overwhelming urge was to head for him to find out exactly why he was here but when I turned to look at Stormie, I found her eyes brimming with tears.

This time, the shoot had truly fallen apart. Stormie knew it. We all knew it.

A voice came from behind me. "Do you have a phone number for Tomie in New York?"

Stormie's eyes grew large and she tilted her head. "Yes."

"Let me talk to him. I can't be on camera, but I am a member of the Director's Guild, and if we've got everything together, we can start shooting now and be finished by the time the blizzard is over. I'm not going anywhere until then and it seems you can use a director who knows what she's doing."

It was Mom.

She stepped forward, looking directly at the camera operator. "It looks like you've got a good set-up. Will you walk me through it? I'm Anna."

"Uh, yeah, sure. I'm Lucas."

"And Darla, thank God you're here. It's the fact we've got a seasoned pro that will get us through this. Can you do interviews and facilitate the filming in the kitchen tonight?"

"Yes. Yes, I can."

"Okay. Let me talk to New York, then you all show me what has to happen to get this show rolling successfully. Also, who's the guy with the dog?" She looked at me. "Did I meet him earlier?"

"Oh. That's Philip Young," said Stormie. "He used to work here."

"Philip Young? The painter?"

"Yeah, I guess so."

I smiled to myself. Stormie, not knowing Philip, was likely remembering that he used to repaint the inn's rooms to keep them fresh.

"And Esther," Mom turned to the production coordinator, "will you make sure everyone is good with hair and make-up, and we've got cameras ready to go in the kitchen, as well as out here?"

"Yes. On it."

The crew, deflated only moments ago, broke off, heading purposefully in different directions. Stormie called Tomie on her cell, which she handed to the new director.

Anna Nash walked off toward the outer hall talking to the producer.

Well, shit.

Did Mom ever not save the day?

"Everyone! Everyone! Final boarding stages!" yelled Esther, and just like that the energy in the room ramped up, the contestants hurrying back to their stations.

I headed for Philip and Whistle.

"Hey," he said.

"What are you doing here? You're supposed to be en route to Boston."

"Funny story," he said. "It looked like we were going to make it out before the storm hits. We were all on board, ready to go. Then the pilot announces the plane is experiencing mechanical difficulties. Flight cancelled."

"Oh, no. I'm sorry."

"There is one more flight to Boston that leaves at six tomorrow morning that would connect me to Paris. There's a slight chance it can be one of the last planes out."

"It's not the same mechanically-challenged plane?"

"No, different airline altogether."

"I don't want you to go, but I know timing is crucial."

"Yeah. The main players in my personal drama are all in Paris now, and in three days, they're not. I'm going to try to make it. If I can't, I can't. Sometimes, life makes the decisions for you."

"And sometimes, it's mechanical difficulties. What about Whistle?"

"I swung by home and picked her up. I wasn't sure where either you or I were going to ride out the storm, but you know how far back the cottage is, and how hard it is to get to. It will surely be at the bottom of Murray's plow-out list. I didn't want her stuck by herself."

"I'm glad you brought her."

Whistle was excited, happy to see me, wanting to leap into my arms to say hello. It's hard not to fall for a pup like that. When I first arrived at MacTavish's, I fell for Whistle first, her owner second.

"Jeff got you the keys?"

"Yes, thanks. Jeff and his cab were still at the airport when the flight was cancelled. He took me back to our place. I grabbed Whistle and drove us here. My car's in employee parking just in case I can catch another flight."

"Okay, that makes sense. Did Jeff tell you about going into your place while I was looking for the keys? Or anything else that happened there?"

Philip looked slightly concerned. "No..."

"While I was trying to find your keys—in a sock, really?—Jeff came in to use the john and fill his water bottle. Which left my mom and this art guy named Leonard Ruskin alone in the car. In any case, by the time I found your keys, the two of them were in your studio. I shooed them out immediately and made sure Leonard didn't take any photos. I'm sorry. I know how you feel about people trespassing in the studio without you, or when things aren't completely organized."

"Ladies and gentlemen! We will be gathering to Zoom with Tomie Lanaro in New York in fifteen minutes. Fifteen! Then we'll be ready to go, according to the schedule you've been given!" This was Esther, the production coordinator.

"Leonard Ruskin was in my studio?" Philip looked startled.

"Yes. Have you heard of him?"

"Everyone in the art world has heard of him. He is an arbiter of taste and of what's coming up. He was in my studio?"

"Yeah. Did you not recognize him when he was talking to Planton at the Battened Hatch?"

"I'm not certain what he looks like, something about a bow tie? Oh, man."

"Why? What's wrong?"

"Most artists would give anything to have him come to their studio. But, not in the state mine is in. I didn't leave it ready for visitors."

"That's why I shooed them out."

"Oh, man."

"If it's any comfort, Ruskin definitely noticed your painting at the Cavalleros'. Planton spoke highly of you."

"Story of my life. Good news, bad news. Someday I'd like to stick the landing on the good news part."

"So, as far as you know, neither Planton or Ruskin are involved in art theft?"

"Far as I know. But thieves don't tend to announce themselves."

"Is it ever okay to sell a painting if the line of ownership isn't completely clean? Or hasn't yet been certified?"

"I think it happens quite often. Ownership can get murky if things are passed down through generations of heirs who don't care or don't know what they have. What happens if you find something in the basement of your family's Flemish castle? Or your uncle goes to prison for insider trading but has all these paintings that came from somewhere?"

"Zoom in ten, folks!" Esther continued the countdown.

"So what's going on? Is the gingerbread contest still happening?" Philip asked.

"Possibly."

"Yes. Yes, it is." And there was my mother, my businesslike mother, next to us, seemingly fresh as a daisy at ten p.m. She extended her hand to Philip, who had to move Whistle to his other arm to shake it. "I'm Anna. I know we met earlier. I'm now directing this gingerbread extravaganza. And I hear you're the man."

Philip's face lit up. He forgot about his cancelled flight and the trouble awaiting him in Paris, for a moment anyway. "Philip Young. And yes, I guess I am the man. At least, I'm the very fortunate one who is in love with your daughter. Well, living with your daughter. We are each other's significant others."

Oh shit.

Mom wasn't expecting this but she can soldier on after anything. "And your painting. One of the most memorable parts of visiting the Cavalleros house. Anyway! What are you doing for the next four or five hours? I've noticed how you connect with the contestants. You even calmed down the woman in the dirndl earlier today."

"Gretl Haus."

"Yes. Is she really German, by the way?"

"Kind of? Not really? You need to stand out in some kind of way to make it onto these shows. But don't give her away."

Mom made the sign of zipped lips. "Here's what I need. I need someone who enjoys talking to people, who can prep each contestant and then interview them. You'd be off camera, we'd only hear your voice. But the answers would be used as an intro to the contestant and also for voiceover when needed. You'd be paid, of course."

"Did not see this request coming. But I do need something to concentrate on other than the blizzard for the next few hours. Why not? But you wouldn't have to pay me."

"Yes, we would," said Anna Nash. "And you'll need to sign a contract. Come talk to me for five minutes about the kinds of questions we need, then I'm handing you over to Esther for the contract and Lucas to get these interviews done."

As she guided Philip past me, he dumped Whistle into my arms. "Her stuff is over there," he said.

Then Mom walked by me and though she didn't pause, her eyes said everything that could possibly be said about me living with a guy who happened to be an astonishing painter, a situation I wasn't mentioning but she found fabulously interesting and she'd *talk to me later*.

I took the opportunity to bring Whistle back to suite seven and leave her there with water and her bed. She first met Philip at Mac-Tavish's and was used to hanging out while he repainted the rooms. She did a couple of circles and collapsed onto her bed, tired from all the recent attention.

Ten minutes later, in the double ballrooms, everyone gathered around the monitor to talk with Tomie Lanaro, the producer in New York City. He seemed businesslike and relieved that things were finally on track. He was short and toned with a pulsing energy. I was glad he was overseeing this from a distance. Folks would likely remain calmer.

Glenn MacTavish, the inn's owner, joined the group. He wore full Scottish regalia: kilt, sporran, tuxedo shirt, Bonnie Prince Charlie jacket and vest, bow tie. He was tall, with reddish hair and full beard, and presented quite the picture.

Once the Zoom was done and the machine that was production started humming, Mom and I followed Stormie and Gretl, the first baker scheduled, to the kitchen.

"Why is Mr. MacTavish here, and in his duds?" I asked Stormie.

"He's a judge."

Ah, that made perfect sense. It would not only add visual interest but would be another way to advertise MacTavish's as the location.

Sven, the second camera operator, was set up to be in the kitchen as each contestant cooked his or her gingerbread, talking the audience through their process, including secrets and tips.

Stormie and crew had done a terrific job of cleaning and setting up the part of the kitchen where the gingerbread would be made. Gretl's ingredients awaited, as did mixing bowl and an industrial mixer.

"Can you stand behind the table, please, so I can get final readings?" asked Sven.

Gretl complied, checking her list against the items before her. Then she picked up a wooden spoon and stood still, smiling at Sven. It was the first time I'd seen her smile. It wasn't completely convincing.

Mom said, "Gretl, you're going to talk Darla through exactly what you're doing to make successful gingerbread."

"Yes," said Gretl. "Correct."

"We are ready," said Darla, coming to stand near Gretl.

"Great. I see the schedule gave you an hour to mix it and put it in the oven, but the mixing won't take that long, surely?"

"No. I'm very efficient. I will have it in the oven in fifteen minutes."

"Great. We'll give you half an hour and then we'll have the next baker ready to go. Sven, you good? Stormie, everything look good to you? The oven is heated?"

"Yes."

"Then, ladies and gentlemen, this is the official start. Sven, give Marla the cue when you're ready. Ms. Haus, please introduce yourself and start mixing."

"*Guten tag*," said Gretl. But before she could finish her sentence, the kitchen door swung open.

"Stop! Stop right now! What the holy hell is going on?" a voice roared from the entrance.

We spun around to find Chef Angelica in a heavy coat, her cheeks red from the cold, standing in the middle of the kitchen.

HELL BREAKS LOOSE

Ingredients

1.5 oz vanilla vodka
1 oz ginger liqueur such as Domaine de Canton
1 tsp molasses
1 oz heavy cream or half and half
Pinch of ground cinnamon
Pinch of nutmeg
1 tbsp of raw honey
Gingerbread cookies
Small plate
Cocktail strainer
Martini glass
Ice
Cocktail shaker

Method

Beforehand, put martini glass in freezer to chill.
Crush gingerbread cookies.
Put honey onto small plate, separately add cookies.
Take frozen martini glass and moisten the rim with a little honey and then dip into crushed gingerbread cookies.
Add ice, vanilla vodka, ginger liqueur, molasses, and heavy cream to cocktail shaker and shake for about 20 seconds until all ingredient are combined and you have created a nice smooth velvety texture.
Strain over martini glass and add pinch of cinnamon and nutmeg for garnish.

15

TOO MANY COOKS

"Chef!" exclaimed Stormie.

"What the hell is going on here? What have you done? Meet me in the lobby. Now."

Stormie looked at me in desperation. I went out with her. Mom followed to see exactly how this was going to play out.

Chef Angelica cornered Stormie by the wall. "I know what you're doing. I know you've always wanted to take my place, have the top job! But this is really too far. It's bad enough to come back and find you've taken over my kitchen and rented it out for some cockamamie television show. My kitchen! That stops, *now*. You waited for me to leave for the Brewster Competition and you moved in and took over!"

"There are six bakers. They're making gingerbread dough. They'll be out of the kitchen in three hours. I didn't think it was a big deal."

Uh-oh. Even I knew that last sentence should somehow be taken back.

"Not. A. Big. Deal?" Angelica's eyes bored through to the back of Stormie's skull. "You are so fired!" She took a step forward.

Instead of stepping back, Stormie stood tall. She shook out her hair.

"I don't think so," she said. "I don't think you're going to fire me."

The two women stood locked in a death stare.

"This is a boon for MacTavish's and will bring a lot of good publicity. The kitchen will be completely reset before breakfast," said Stormie.

"If it's such a great thing, why did you do it behind my back? That is total subordination!"

"If I had told you, would you have facilitated it?"

"Of course not."

"There you have it."

"Now then, Lassie—er, Chef." This was spoken by Glenn. "So good to see you back. Come, let's talk for a moment."

Chef Angelica was still breathing fire. But Glenn owned the place. Did she quit and walk? Or did she comply?

"We'll have some privacy in my office," Glenn said, and Angelica Dormer turned on her heel and followed him back.

"Well," said Mom. "That's a thing."

Stormie was trembling. Mom grabbed her shoulders. "Go back. Tell Gretl and Darla that Angelica is excitable, but everything is fine. Then start shooting. Shoot as many bakers as quickly as you can."

Stormie nodded. Mom headed for Glenn's office at a brisk pace.

I stood in the lobby. My eyes once again fixed on the settee, which still had crime scene tape around it and a police blanket thrown over the spot where Noel Schlessinger sat.

"Hi. Avalon, is it?"

I turned to find Professor Jules Eckhardt beside me. "You're Anna Nash's daughter?"

"Yes."

"She texted me that she'd like to meet. I answered a while ago but haven't heard back. I'm about to turn in for the night. If you see her, would you ask her if she can join me for breakfast in the morning? Or really, just have her check her messages."

"Sure. She has unexpectedly taken over directing the gingerbread contest for the Delicious Network."

"Not surprised."

"I'll let her know."

"I'm heading back to my room. I just saw Leonard Ruskin. I don't want to talk to him. I hope he hasn't realized who I am."

With that, she vanished into the far halls.

No sooner had she gone than Clementine Patterson, the make-up person, fluttered into the lobby. She still wore a flowing patchwork skirt with metallic gold stripes woven through. She had pulled a green sweater over her crepe top. All she was missing was a sign reading "Woodstock or Bust."

She recognized me as tangential to the shoot. "Hi. Have you seen—"

At that point, Mom came striding from the hall to Glenn's office, Chef Angelica in tow. "Clementine, here she is, our final judge! I need her ready within about an hour. Is that possible?"

Clementine grasped Chef Angelica's chin and thoughtfully turned to different ways in the light. "Yes, yes. You're not wearing this though, certainly?"

"No, she'll be wearing her chef's coat or a nice outfit," said the director. "I'll leave you two to firm up the details."

"Yes, yes," said Clementine. "A chef's coat will do—unless you have an outstanding dress available? Something that will read well if you're standing next to the Scotsman?"

The two of them made plans. Clementine headed back to her post.

Chef Angelica stood next to me. I'd never seen her at a loss before.

Finally, her eyes focused. "What's that?" she asked me.

"What?"

"The yellow tape. On the sofa there."

"On the banquette settee?"

She glared.

"Crime scene tape. That's where the bounty hunter was killed."

"Bounty hunter? Killed?"

"Yes. Yesterday. It was a hit."

"A hit? Here?"

I nodded.

"You're sure it was a bounty hunter?"

"Yes. Noel Schlessinger. From Ossining."

Chef Angelica went white, considerably more than normal. She looked like she might throw up. She somehow regained her aplomb and stalked away.

The night manager dimmed the lobby lights slightly. As he did, a loudspeaker came on. It was one that didn't go into the rooms but could be heard throughout the inn's lobby and hallways. "Ladies and gents, we've just been informed by the local state police that due to the impending storm, the mountain passes have been closed. Local traffic should be kept to necessary travel only. Snuggle in, folks. We'll keep you updated."

Such an announcement took me back to the olden days when folks depended on updates from outside sources. Now, everyone was certainly following blizzard updates on their phones.

So, were the bad guys long gone by now and we could all 'snuggle in'? Or were they about to be snowed in among us?

TOO MANY COOKS

Ingredients

1 oz pistachio cream liqueur
1 oz pistachio cello
Fresh strawberries to make two ounces of juice
Fresh strawberries sliced for garnish
Ice
Cocktail shaker
Crushed pistachios for garnish
Collins glass

Method

Blend strawberries and strain juice. Set aside.
Fill collins glass halfway with ice. Gently pour pistachio cream liqueur into
bottom layer of glass over ice. Next continue to gently pour strawberry juice over the
back of a spoon close to the pistachio liqueur to create the next layer. Carefully layer the
pistachio cello on top of the strawberry juice using the same spoon technique.
Garnish cocktail with fresh sliced strawberries and a sprinkle of fresh crushed pistachios on top.
Serve immediately.

16

MUTED COLORS

Semi-darkness made the lobby feel as if we'd traveled back in time, to the 1940s perhaps, when colors were muted and people moved more slowly—though according to the noir films at the time, half of them were up to no good.

Wondering if we were about to be snowed in with a murderer had me spooked.

Being enveloped in the soft, thick scent of gingerbread gave me a discordant feeling of being safe yet in a great amount of danger, like being locked in your grandmother's cedar chest with no way out.

Needing to be around lights and people, I headed back to the set. I passed Emelia and Marta on their way to the kitchen, with Emelia next in line to bake and cool her final gingerbread.

Once in the ballrooms, I didn't even look for Mom. I was sure she had everything humming along. She clearly had a knack for orchestrating the set. Did she want to give up acting to become a director? We never discussed it. We never discussed a lot of things.

Instead, I looked for Philip. He was off in a corner with one of the two male contestants. They were conversing and laughing, like old friends. In his normal state, Philip came off confident yet humble, happy to get to know you, ready to calm and steady you, if needed. Since he wasn't on camera, his thick hair was tousled, his shirt open an extra button because he was near a bank of hot lights. The two of them finished talking and then followed the production coordinator back to the baker's workstation. The baker was miked, with a final make-up check. He got back to work on his creation while answering the questions Philip was posing. I couldn't hear a thing, but it seemed to be going well.

It struck me then that they were going to be shooting into the early hours of the morning—until union rules facilitated rest for the crew.

It also occurred to me that I hadn't gotten much sleep the night before. I was fading fast.

Philip's interview ended. Before he found his next victim, I crossed the room and put a hand on his shoulder. He turned. Then he smiled.

"Mom's in suite seven, and Whistle is there now. The couch in the living room folds out. I'm going to go and try to get some sleep. Come find me when you're done."

"I will." He touched my hair, all that was needed to send a shiver from my shoulders to my feet.

"Is tomorrow morning's flight still on? Where is the blizzard?"

"Storm's heading this way, but the plane is still scheduled to leave at five-thirty a.m. It's anybody's guess."

"Thanks for helping out."

"I really like—" He stopped himself and looked at me, cha-grined.

"You were going to say you really like my mom, weren't you?"

"You told me so."

As I walked through the lobby toward the private hallway for suite seven, Sous Chef Stormie emerged from Pepper's Bistro. It was closed, of course; she was taking a break from the kitchen. Whoever this producer guy Tomie was, I hoped he was worth her stress.

She saw me. We collapsed together into armchairs against the windowed wall, which now faced intense blackness. The moon was hidden behind a thick veil of clouds. There was not a flake to be seen. How different it must have been to live before modern storm tracking and radar. Would you go to bed assuming tomorrow would be a normal day? Or were there people then, such as Jeff the Cabbie, who could feel snow a-comin'?

It didn't take Stormie and me long to realize we were seated across from, therefore staring at, the settee. When the crime scene tape came off, it would likely be junked. Not only was blood famously hard to destain, who would want the reminder of such an act of violence in the middle of the lobby?

"I always liked that banquette settee," I said. "I'll miss it."

Stormie laughed. "Dear God, what a day," she said.

"How is it going in the kitchen? Is the gingerbread almost all baked?"

"Yes. Two more."

"So… what was going on with Chef Angelica? There seems to be some tension between the two of you."

Stormie gave a deep sigh.

"Chef thought I blabbed something she told me in confidence." She laughed. "Something she told me when we'd been drinking—her more than me."

"Yeah? What did she think you'd spilt?"

"It's probably not a secret anymore, given the current situation, but you still have to promise not to tell anyone who told you."

"Double promise."

Stormie's head fell back. The heat from the kitchen was making the curls tighter in her hair. It glistened. She was perspiring—though from baking or tension, I did not know.

I waited.

"Her name isn't really Anglica Dormer. It's Leslie Vandervere."

There was a pause. Stormie continued. "Her name is Leslie Vandervere. There's a warrant out for her arrest."

MUTED COLORS

Ingredients

2 oz dry gin
1 ½ oz fresh squeezed blood orange juice
¾ oz simple syrup
½ oz fresh lemon juice
1 egg white
Dash of orange bitters
Blood orange slice for garnish
Ice
Cocktail shaker
Cocktail strainer
Nick and Nora glass

Method

Chill cocktail glass in freezer and pull out just as you are about to pour your cocktail.
Add ice, dry gin, blood orange juice, simple syrup, fresh lemon juice, and one egg white to cocktail shaker. Shake vigorously for about 20 seconds to create a nice foamy cocktail. Strain and pour into chilled Nick and Nora glass. Finish with a few drops of orange bitters and slice of fresh blood orange.

17

NO DANGER

"*THERE'S A WARRANT out for her?*" I hissed. "For what?"

"She never said."

"But you didn't tell anyone—did you?"

"I want to be head chef, Avalon, but I want it on my own merits. Not because I ratted someone out."

"You didn't call Noel Schlessinger."

"Hell, no."

"You don't think Angelica could kill someone? Specifically, was she willing to kill Noel? I know she acted like she wasn't here until early this morning but..."

"I don't think she killed Noel. I don't think she was here earlier than when we saw her come in. I don't believe she is emotionally able to be here, aware we were shooting a television show in her kitchen, without stopping it. No."

We sat. What should I do? Should I call Inspector Mike Spaulding? Even if I couldn't tell him where the information came from, if he ran the name Leslie Vandervere, he would find some interesting information.

Although, in running background new checks on everyone, had Glenn MacTavish uncovered this himself? Did he have his own plan for dealing with her? Or, now that I knew, was it on me to do something?

Still, nobody was going anywhere tonight.

As the two of us sat, I started to nod off.

"I've gotta go," Stormie finally said. "Gotta get the kitchen shoot finished."

"Hell of a day," I said.

We both stood, then headed opposite directions.

A new security man sat in Mom's hall. This one had a chair, but he was wide awake. As I passed, he took an AirPod out of one ear.

"Audio book?" I asked.

"Podcast. You are?"

I gave my name and was relieved to find I was on his list.

As I entered Mom's hotel suite, I seriously contemplated opening the Champagne all by myself.

Instead, after being happily greeted by Whistle, I opened the sliding door and the pup and I went out onto the terrace. It was very cold.

I was so tired I couldn't think straight. I'd call Mike tomorrow when I knew what to tell him.

The next thing I knew, it was daylight, albeit grey light, and I was asleep under the covers on the pull-out couch.

As I slowly roused, my hand crossed crisp white sheets to the empty pillow where Philip was supposed to be.

Out of habit, I reached down for Whistle, who by rights should be snuggled against my leg.

She was not there.

I pulled myself into a sitting position and checked my watch. It was ten a.m. I'd gone to bed at three-thirty. A pretty good amount of sleep, given the circumstances.

I pulled myself up, then out of bed and over to the sliding doors, where I opened the drapes a scootch.

Ah. Here, at last, was the promised blizzard. Snow was everywhere, on the terrace, on the ice on the lake, blowing sideways through the air. There may have been four inches, but it was blowing around so extravagantly it was hard to know.

The door to Mom's bedroom was closed. I opened it a few inches, just enough to see she was in there, sleeping, and her chest rose and fell—she was alive. Good, good.

As I pulled the door back shut, my phone vibrated.

It was Philip.

I crossed the living room, turned on the gas fireplace and chose a loveseat in front of it. "Good morning," I said. "Where are you?"

"Boston. I'm sitting on the plane to Paris. They're flying planes out as fast as they can as the blizzard approaches. I barely made it out of Tranquility. We're pushing back from the gate now, so I've only got a minute."

"Mon Dieu!"

"When it looked like the five-thirty flight would actually leave, I decided to try for it. I took the car to our place to shower and change. Whistle wanted to come, so I grabbed her. When I got to Boston, I called Noah next door. He's going to feed Whistle later today and let her out in case you're tied up at MacTavish's. He'll shovel us out after the storm. Murray with the snowplow will come by, also."

"Got it, thanks."

"We're second in line for takeoff, so I've got to go. I'll call you when I get to France. Stay safe. Don't do anything crazy. Let the authorities figure this one out, okay?"

"I'll do my best."

"Love you, Av."

"Love you, too."

And he was gone.

Damn.

I didn't know my next move, but I did know from experience that it's always good to be showered and clean in times of natural disaster. Thankfully, I had a fresh pair of bartender's blacks in the pub's storeroom that I could change into, as mine had been slept in. Although, truth be told, bartender blacks are pretty forgiving.

Fortunately, the hotel's plastic laundry bag fit perfectly over my cast. It even had a handy-dandy pull-string. I wouldn't mind the cast itself getting all wet and falling off, but I didn't want to ruin the painting, especially with Philip gone.

I emerged from the suite's guest bathroom to find a room service cart had magically appeared. The spread was a cornucopia of break-fast items: fruit, pastries, sausages, yogurt parfait, an omelet, waffles with strawberry topping, eggs Benedict. There was a pot of coffee and one of hot water with a selection of tea bags. Cranberry juice and fresh squeezed orange juice sat side by side.

Had Mom ordered all this? If so, where was she? Eggs Benedict has a shelf life of thirty seconds.

"Hey, Kiddo." Mom appeared at the bedroom door as if I'd conjured her. She wore pajamas—a top and pants, soft bamboo fabric, a soft pink with a pattern of scrolls. She looked like she was a 1940s movie star, about to play a scene with Rock Hudson or Cary Grant.

I was a mess with wet hair wearing a walking cast and laundry bag under a robe provided by the hotel.

"Hi," I said, "Did you order breakfast?"

"No, I did not." She walked over to check it out.

Of course she didn't order it. For one thing, she's a vegetarian so she wouldn't have ordered the meats.

We stood there looking at the embarrassment of choices and both realized at the same moment: we were starving.

She handed me a plate and took one herself and we each loaded them up. She grinned and brought the cart over to where the sofa was still folded out. She folded the brown comforter in half and we plunked down, using it as a picnic blanket. I took the opportunity to pull the plastic bag off the cast as I heaved it up.

There are some perks to being famous. People send you stuff. Sometimes you take advantage.

"So how did the shoot go?" I asked, to make conversation. "What's up with Chef Angelica?"

"Chef Angelica is going to be treated as a famous chef who is judging the contest. Step one: calm her ego. Step two, get her on your side."

"Did you know Angelica Dormer isn't her real name?"

Mom's blue eyes widened. "I did know. How did you know?"

"I have informants around here," I said. "How did you find out?"

"Glenn MacTavish told me after she'd left his office. Glenn and the Chef have agreed they will talk to local law enforcement after the show is finished and the blizzard has passed. She promised to resolve her issues with the outstanding warrants. She says they're not serious."

"So she says," I said, cutting off a bite of eggs Benedict. Whoever was in the kitchen this morning made a heck of a hollandaise.

"Is it always this interesting around these parts?"

"Somehow, yes," I said, and I started laughing.

She laughed too, first a giggle and then hoots.

When we finally pulled ourselves together, she went to make herself a cup of tea. "You want some coffee?" she asked, nodding to the cast I'd hiked up onto the bed.

"Yes, please," I said. Of course, she remembered how I like it without having to ask.

"What's the deal with your cast? It's the most impressive one I've ever seen."

"Oh. Philip painted it." No use pretending I didn't know him.

"You might be the only one in the world with a cast that's an original Philip Young."

"Still can't wait to get the damn thing off."

"Do you have cream to put on the places it's rubbed?"

"Yeah. Thanks."

"This food is very tasty."

"It is—but weren't you supposed to have breakfast with Jules Eckhardt?"

"I was. I texted her after I woke up. Haven't heard back."

She sat back on the bed and sipped her tea, then closed her eyes and inhaled the aroma. Lady Grey, one of her favorite blends I knew it well.

It's hard not to love Anna Nash when she's sitting on the bed in her pajamas being entranced by the taste and aroma of tea. No make-up, straight hair, eyes light blue-grey instead of the arresting ocean-blue so many of her costumes bring out. She could easily be

a romantic lead rather than a comedic actor. Yet there's no deny-
ing she's an insanely talented comedian. There's little she won't try.
Unlike the romantic leads, she's willing to do whatever it takes for
a laugh or to be in character. It sounds petty, but I hate it when she
makes herself look comic. I don't mind so much when she wears
wigs and costumes and disappears into another character but I hate
it when she makes grotesque faces or uses false teeth. It makes me
uncomfortable, like she's not really herself. Petty feelings, like I said.

"Are you open to talking about Philip? He did a good job with
the background interviews with the bakers."

All I could manage was a heavy sigh. "Do you really think you
can complete the episode? When do you start shooting the rest of
it?"

"Thanks to Stormie, all the bakers completed their final bakes
overnight. This will be the fun part, watching them put it all
together. We start up again at noon. I sure hope we'll have power to
carry us through the shoot."

"MacTavish's has a monster generator. You should be all right."

"It seems the blizzard has started."

"Yes. Philip flew to Boston at five-thirty this morning on the last
flight out. He called from the flight to Paris, which was ready for
takeoff. According to FlightAware, it is now somewhere over the
Atlantic, well ahead of the storm."

"Ah. I'm getting the feeling you're not thrilled I'm doing this.
Helping finish the shoot."

I wasn't going to say anything. This is the kind of thing I usually
keep bottled up. But, when asked directly... "Why did you do it?
You were here to talk to me about family stuff. Now you're shooting
a gingerbread house contest."

"A lot of people were invested in it. They'd travelled here. They'd
worked for months on their houses. Or they were local crew members who'd been hired by the Delicious Network, about to lose a
piece of their livelihood. It seemed a good use of two days of my

time. The ship had a crew and the passengers were on board. All they needed was a captain."

"I know," I said softly. And I did know. She had a big heart and a steel spine. "It's just…" And here I was, about to sound petty out loud. "When you leave, Anna Nash will morph into a local legend. As always."

"Yeah?"

"You know it. That's who you are. You're always willing to put yourself out there for anyone who needs help. The marginalized, the defenseless, or regular old crew members and the freaking normal people who want to build gingerbread houses."

My anger gathered into a ball, rose into my throat and pushed hot tears from my eyes.

"Couldn't you just fucking do it somewhere else? Anywhere else? This was my town. The place I was Avalon, for better or worse. Love me or hate me. I was myself. Avalon.

"Now that's all gone. Like it always is. From now on, I'll be Avalon Nash, daughter of Anna Nash, A-list Hollywood actor and Tranquility legend. No one will look at me the same way. They already don't. Your shadow has arrived. And your shadow is as big as the cloud banks that cover the mountain peaks surrounding this town. My whole life is now under cloud cover."

She sat, holding her tea. I couldn't read her expression.

"It's like you picked them off one by one. Marta, my barback. Sous Chef Stormie, my friend. Glenn MacTavish, my boss. And Philip. You sucked him into your orbit like a tractor beam. He will never look at me again without seeing the residual fairy dust of you."

Silence hung thick between us.

Wind howled outside, rattling the French doors.

Finally, she spoke. "Fairy dust?"

Now there was a lot going on behind her eyes. I couldn't read the exact mix of emotions.

But I'd gotten up a head of steam. "You had personal stuff, family stuff you needed to talk to me about. You couldn't come into town quietly, ask to stay with me, we talk about stuff, you head out. You couldn't do that. You had to book a room at my place of business and turn up in my pub. You had to save the day by directing a cooking show.

"And worse. Worse! An art theft investigator comes into town to work with the local authorities because there is a dangerous, decades-old, billion-dollar crime ring about to be brought down, and you couldn't just watch, you had to get involved! You had to put your life on the line for no good reason at all! Why do you do that? Why do you walk into the highest-profile situations? There are rapists waiting in your hotel rooms, and people with billions to lose knowing you're onto them? How am I supposed to keep you safe?"

"Okay," she said. "That's a lot.

"Yes, there was a disturbed person in my hotel room. Believe it or not, there usually isn't one. As far as the art theft, what can I say? Jules Eckhardt is an interesting person. Kind of like a real-life Indiana Jones. College professor by day, art crusader on her time off. She has gotten fancy museums to return bones of indigenous peoples. Now, she's helping the authorities close in on a ring of thieves that's somehow operated under the radar for decades. Decades! Isn't that interesting?"

"Have you ever met someone who wasn't interesting?"

She chewed her croissant, contemplating. "Silly? Yes. Working against their own best interests? Many people. Downright mean or purposefully misinformed? Yes, indeed. Heroic in ways they themselves don't even realize? Those are my favorite people. But someone who's not interesting? No. I haven't met that person. Yet."

"It doesn't matter to me how interesting Jules Eckhardt is, or how much danger she wades into. She is not my mother. You are. So please, don't be Indiana Jones. Please. Someone got shot. We're not sure the assassin left, or who hired them, or why. It may have been a one-off that has nothing to do with anyone at the hotel. Or it could. And the assassin could still be here, snowed in with us."

"I understand," Mom replied, her voice calm and steady. "I really think the danger has passed. The main thing you need to know is, it isn't your job to keep me safe. That's on me. But I'll finish up directing this small, one-off episode about gingerbread houses and I'll keep my head down.

"Also, people from art theft rings don't usually go offing a potential client. No one knows I'm onto them, that I know the authorities are closing in. At the moment, I just hope Jules knows I've tried to get ahold of her and haven't stood her up somehow."

Mom got out her phone and looked through her text messages. She shook her head. Jules hadn't answered her morning text.

"Oh, wait," she said, pulling down another notification. "Jules called and left a message." She punched in the code to retrieve her voicemail and put it on speaker.

"Hi, Anna, it's Jules. I went ahead and had breakfast. I'm back in my room. If you've got a minute, we can grab a cup of coffee? I'm curious about what you have to tell me about your boat trip with Leonard Ruskin. Speaking of Mr. Ruskin, wait till you hear what I just found out!"

In the background, we heard a knocking. "Oh, wait. Is that you, Anna? If so, perfect timing."

A few seconds of walking, then some fumbling with the phone as Jules freed her hands to open the locks on her hotel room door. "Hello! Wait. Wait. Wait."

A gunshot.

The sound of a body dropping to the ground.

Then, the sound of a hotel room door swinging shut.

NO DANGER

Mocktail

Ingredients

4 sprigs basil
4 sprigs mint
½ cup fresh orange juice
¼ cup fresh lemon juice
¼ cup fresh lime juice
1 teaspoon fresh agave nectar
1 pinch of ground cayenne pepper
1 pinch turmeric
Fresh wedge of lime for garnish
Splash of sparkling water to finish cocktail
Ice
Pint glass
Cocktail shaker
Cocktail strainer

Method

Add juices to cocktail shaker with ice, agave nectar, and pinch of cayenne and turmeric. Rip the leaves of both mint and basil and add to shaker, saving some mint aside. Shake all ingredients together and pour into cocktail glass. Top off with sparkling water and place lime wedge on side. Lightly bruise the remainer of mint and basil by gently crushing into palms of your hands to help release flavors and float on top of mocktail.

18

OKAY, DANGER

OM AND I stared at each other.

"Fuck," said Mom. "What should we do? Should I call 911?"

"Wait, wait, no. She was here working with Mike Spaulding. Let me see if I can reach him."

I hobbled over to find my phone. I hit the call icon by Mike's number.

Please pick up, please pick up, please pick up…

He answered on the fourth ring, a bit out of breath.

"What is it, Nash? We've got a thing or two going on over here."

"Jules Eckhardt. She's been shot."

"What? Hold on." He took a moment to step away to somewhere quieter.

"Tell me everything. Slowly."

I did.

"Okay, we've got an ambulance on the way. Not sure how long it will take to navigate the roads. I'm heading over to MacTavish's right now. What room is she in?"

"Whiteface 326," said Mom.

"On our way. Keep your line open."

"You weren't kidding when you said it was always interesting around these parts," Mom said. "I guess we'd better get dressed."

"Mom. When did she call?"

"About half an hour ago. That could be what woke me."

"Shit."

"I know."

We were dressed and out the door within five minutes. Philip urged me to stay out of this one. I was trying my best. Truly I was. I just wasn't having much luck.

The lights were fully on in the lobby, washing it in gold against the raging snowstorm outside the floor-to-ceiling windows. The lake had already disappeared.

Nelson, head of security, was on his walkie-talkie.

"Are they here yet?" I asked.

"Almost," he said, correctly guessing to whom I referred. His body was wired with energy. He stood by the revolving front door, as if to hurry the authorities to us.

"Nelson, has anyone gone to Jules' room? We have to get to her."

"No. The police and ambulance are almost here."

"We can't leave her alone a second more than necessary. Come on," Mom said.

Nelson left his security assistant Naomi to wait for the ambulance and state police as the three of us rushed into the side hall that led to the long corridor to Jules Eckhardt's room.

Once there, Mom banged on the door. "Jules! Jules, it's us! Can you hear me?"

No answer.

Nelson moved past and put the skeleton key into the lock. Mac-Tavish's had chosen not to go to electronic card readers.

Jules Eckhardt had unlocked the door from the inside before she'd been shot. Nelson pushed it open six inches. "Ms. Eckhardt, are you here?"

And then we heard a groan. Not a loud noise, but a distinctly human one

"I don't want to hurt you. I'm going to try to open the door wide enough to come in. Help is on the way."

Nelson was able to push the heavy wooden door a bit farther, enough space for him to step through. Mom, who undoubtedly felt guilty for not seeing her voice message, squeezed in behind.

What was I supposed to do?

If it had seemed obvious she was dead, I would have waited in the hall. My ability to deal with corpses was already brimming. No more.

Still, once the authorities arrived, I knew I wouldn't be allowed anywhere close. I entered the room.

The curtains across by the sliding doors were open, wind shuddering the glass. The desk lamp was on, spilling a muted burst of light.

Jules Eckhardt lay on the thick forest green carpet on the floor, on her back. Blood pooled beneath and behind her. I stepped over her still form to be out of the way. I expected more blood. Couldn't you bleed out in half an hour?

Mom was instantly down on her knees. "Jules! Can you hear me?"

Jules' eyes opened.

"It's Anna. I'm sorry I didn't get your message, but we're here now, and an ambulance is on the way. Did you see who did this? Who shot you?"

"Red hair," Jules whispered. "Electric red."

Nelson and I exchanged knowing glances. "Leggings? Possibly tight black pants?" he asked.

"I think." It was clear Jules wasn't in a position to hold a conversation.

"Be still until they get here. We've got you now," Mom reassured her.

As she said that, a tromping of the troops was heard in the hallway.

A crisp knock at the door. Nelson opened it as far as possible. Inspector Mike Spaulding entered first. He wore a heavy navy blue virga jacket with a faux fur collar and lots of pockets. Usually, he was completely in civilian clothes, but it was a blizzard.

Mom stepped back over Jules and stood next to me.

Soon the room was filled with state police officers and EMTs. "Can I listen to the message?" Mike asked.

"Oh," I said. "Inspector Spaulding, this is my mother, Anna Nash."

"Got it," he said.

Another friend who'd look at me differently, going forward.

She cued the message and let him listen to the phone privately.

"Okay. Do we have your permission to request this message from your phone network provider? It would save us having to get a warrant."

"Yes, of course."

Nelson came straight over to Spaulding. "She said she was shot by someone in a red wig," he said. "Red wig and black leggings. Sounds like a repeat offender."

"She said she was shot by someone with electric red hair and the person could have been wearing black pants or leggings," Mom corrected.

The EMTs had a wheeled stretcher down on the ground next to Jules. They'd assessed her wound and staunched any blood flow. In a practiced move, two of them lifted her onto the gurney and pulled it up to waist height.

Mike grabbed Jules' purse, briefcase, and phone and prepared to follow her out.

Mom and I also left the room behind the stretcher. The EMTs stopped in the hall to tighten straps across Jules and pull a sheet across her chest. "Good thing you found her when you did," one of them said to Mom. "Another half an hour and the roads might have been impassable, even for us."

"Good thing."

Mom leaned over Jules and said, "Take care. We'll come to see you as soon as we can." Jules nodded ever so slightly. Then, in a low voice meant only for Jules to hear, Mom said, "The red-haired woman who shot you. Did she have a five o'clock shadow?"

Jules eyes popped open at that. And she nodded.

OKAY, DANGER

Ingredients

2 oz bourbon
1 oz lemon juice
1 oz black current juice
½ oz maple syrup
1 oz aquafaba (chickpea juice, strain one can)
Dash of angostura bitters
Pinch of ground cinnamon
Cinnamon stick for garnish
Ice
Cocktail shaker
Rocks glass

Method

In cocktail shaker add ice, bourbon, lemon juice, black current juice, maple syrup, aquafaba, angostura bitters and pinch of fresh ground cinnamon. Shake vigorously for about 30 seconds until you have a nice frothy cocktail. Pour through cocktail strainer into rocks glass. Add ice to finish cocktail along with a pinch of cinnamon and one cinnamon stick for garnish.

19

SUSPECT EVERYONE

Not surprisingly, Glenn MacTavish was in the lobby as they packed Jules into the waiting ambulance. The EMTs weren't kidding about how bad the roads were. I hoped they'd make it to the hospital without incident.

Glenn wore jeans and an olive green sweater. He clearly hadn't expected to be seen in public just yet. I took the opportunity to tell him I didn't think the Battened Hatch could open, as Marta was spoken for and Manuela had texted that she couldn't get out her front door. We agreed that If Pepper's could stay open for the guests sheltering in place at the hotel, we'd be okay.

"Oh, and if you sent the breakfast cart this morning, thank you," I said. I didn't know anyone else who had the authority to present such a gourmet feast during a snowstorm. Well, except Stormie.

But Glenn took responsibility. "You and me and our moms," he said.

"Crazy, hunh?"

Few people knew that Pepper Porter, the golden age movie star, was actually Glenn's biological mother. I did know. Now he knew about mine. As far as Glenn was concerned, we were both sprinkled with Famous Mom Fairy Dust.

Nothing to be done. Qué será, será.

After the excitement, Anna Nash and I repaired to the still locked and closed Battened Hatch. I kept the lights off in the main room, to not give false hope to possible patrons. I put on the lights behind and over the bar and turned on the stepped colored lights under the bottles, just to show off. At the moment, they were gold and green.

"I'm going to the storeroom to change into some fresh clothes," I said. "Want anything to drink before I go? Tea? Whisky?"

"Tea, if possible."

I ducked into the kitchen, which was pristine, glowing, and busy as it would be for any breakfast service. Obviously, some of the line cooks had been persuaded to bunk at the hotel to ride out the blizzard.

I was able to wrangle Mom a large cup of tea and a chai latte for myself from Pepper's barista. Then I headed back to the storeroom.

When I opened the door, it took only seconds to realize something was different. Only seconds, because the room was no longer dark. Light was coming from the far reaches.

"Hello?" I said. Who could have gotten the keys? I had a set and hotel security had a set.

I re-opened the hall door and turned on the overhead light so I could make a run for it if necessary. Then I walked foot by foot across the front of the room. No one seemed to be there.

"Hello?"

I sidled along the wall to the back. Still no one. Then I turned a corner to find a very handsome art deco-style floor lamp. There was a note Scotch taped to the base.

Carefully, I walked over.

Thought you might like this. I'll work on the chair and the rug when I get back. –P

Damn. How thoughtful of him.

I'd nearly had a heart attack.

I quieted my breathing and pulled on fresh clothes. Okay, I admit I wore the same pants, because I wanted to ruin as few pairs as possible by cutting the lower leg to make room for the damn cast.

I turned off the lamp, put the note into my pocket to make me smile, and headed back.

It felt oddly familiar to have Anna Nash at her usual spot at the bar looking at her phone.

"Hey, look at this," she said. She turned her phone to me. A text was on it, recipient Tomie Lanaro, producer of the gingerbread show. Mom had attached a photo. "*Is this your director Will Acton?*"

"Hell, no!" was Tomie's response.

Mom's phone rang. The producer's voice could be heard even without speaker being on. "Did that guy say he was Will? That explains a lot! The real Will said he wasn't even there and I said, yeah, that's how they felt, too. I guess I owe him an apology!"

A sharp rap came at the lobby door. I left the gingerbread director and producer talking and stalked back through the unlit hallway. "Who is it?"

"Mike Spaulding."

Thank goodness.

He came in, melting snow dripping from his coat and hat. He looked like a man who didn't have a cordial relationship with winter.

"You should be flattered, Nash. You're the only civilian whose phone calls I take in the middle of a busy working blizzard."

"Not even Valerie's?" I referenced his girlfriend, whom I liked a lot.

"Perhaps she and I get along so well because she can stay out of trouble."

"Yeah, yeah. I'd say staying out of trouble is overrated, but I'd like to see how it feels first. I'm working on it."

"Not hard enough." He nearly cracked a smile. I motioned to a booth. Each one had a candlestick lamp and I turned one on. Mike saw Anna at the bar and motioned her over. He took off his coat and state police hat and put them onto the booth bench.

Mom completed her call, came over and slid in next to me across from Mike.

"Any word on Jules?" she asked.

"Yes. We're assuming she was shot by the same assassin—by

someone who knew what he or she was doing. Professor Eckhardt was shot in her shoulder. It wasn't a kill, it was a warning."

The shadows cast by the low light made me feel like we were in an old noir movie.

"Speaking of the assassin," Mom said, "who I am none too pleased to realize is still among us, it turns out the man passing himself off as Will Acton, the gingerbread show director, was not Will Acton at all." She turned her phone to Inspector Spaulding.

"May I see it?" Mike took the phone and enlarged the photo Mom had taken of the phony director.

"It does seem the right body type. He's small and thin and I'm thinking tight black jeans could seem like tights on a grainy black and white security camera. We're also looking at this Leonard Ruskin fellow. Apparently, Eckhardt had intel that Ruskin probably won't lead us to the mastermind because he likely *is* the mastermind."

"Holy bananas," said Mom. I don't know where she got that expression from.

"So, I have to tell you—yes, it seems the assassin is among us. And dangerous. In fact, no matter what their role is in this thing, I'd proceed as if both the bogus Will Acton and Leonard Ruskin are armed and dangerous. I'd also be careful, because they're both only suspects. We have no proof. Someone completely different might be our killer. Male, female or otherwise."

"So, suspect everyone?" asked Mom.

"Suspect everyone."

SUSPECT EVERYONE

Mocktail

Ingredients

1 cup fresh brewed chai tea, chilled
¼ cup light cream/milk
2 small scoops of chai gelato/ice cream
Pinch of cinnamon
Pinch of nutmeg
Milkshake spoon
Pint glass

Method

Steep one cup of chai tea and bring to room temperature.
Chill. In pint glass add 2 scoops of chai gelato/ice cream.
Slowly pour ice chai tea over ice cream. Stir in light cream
or milk. Add milkshake spoon and finish with a pinch of
cinnamon and nutmeg.

20
FINAL HOURS

THE FINAL HOURS of the shoot started at noon. I went to watch. I didn't know where else to go when I'd been told to suspect anyone might be an assassin.

It was a closed set, so I had to enter with Mom. I hated using her professional access even in that small way.

Stormie met us at the door to the ballroom. "Tomie told me! Will Acton was not the real Will Acton at all. He was a fake director!"

Esther Ringwald, the production coordinator, was nearby. "I only hope our new director can work with the correct *patina*," she drawled.

We burst into laughter. Mom and Stormie moved off into the room.

I couldn't help but stare again at Esther. Small, petite, red hair.

Suspect everyone.

Jules' shooting hadn't been widely broadcast. Anyone who saw her leave in an ambulance might have thought she had appendicitis. Mike felt the general public wasn't at risk, and besides, he didn't want to cause a panic when everyone was already locked in together.

But did I qualify as "general public"? Did Mom? Or were we people who Leonard Ruskin considered enough of a threat that he would strand us at the Cavalleros house? If Ruskin was, indeed, the ringleader, what was Planton's involvement? Was Ruskin stashing us at Planton's to deal with us later? Or was it that Planton, along with his security guy, were the muscle, and we'd simply never reappear from across the lake?

Yet. Leonard Ruskin had turned the boat around to come get us.

He seemed so... bow-tied, much more likely to be an unwitting pawn in the thieves' game, the go-between who would show rich investors a "red book" filled with paintings of dubious ownership. The kind of guy who would be shocked to discover the paintings were straight-up stolen. Right?

How naïve was I willing myself to be? Jules Eckhardt had been shot in her own hotel room, opening the door, thinking it was a friend knocking.

I decided to stay on the closed set, and not think about Esther's hair. The ballroom chairs had cushioned seats and backs. I found one by a wall and sat. I didn't want to be noticed. I certainly didn't want to help out. Thankfully, I knew Mom wouldn't ask me.

It was two thirty four p.m. when the power went out all over Tranquility

The town, already darkened by a barrage of white driving snow, became pewter. It's always an odd feeling when it's dark out during the day. Only the streetlamps, which had solar panels, would remain on until they ran out of stored sunlight.

A loud, collective groan rose from cast and crew, followed by what sounded like an orchestrated sigh of relief when the generator kicked in and the lights returned.

Anna Nash was a natural director. She kept things moving along. She had good ideas and was happy to hear those of other people. In this case, she kept people who were under pressure on an even keel. It took a while to reshoot the set-up that was in progress when the electricity went off, but she kept it going.

Afterwards, contestants and crew took a break. Thanks to Stormie, there was a nice spread for lunch.

Mom announced that the gingerbread house creators, who were nearly finished, would have an hour for final touches once the cameras rolled again. Until then, they needed to step away from their tables. She suggested they eat and use the rest room.

It was clear that everyone, crew included, was eager to finish.

I let the cast and crew have first go at the food. To quell my nerves, I decided to embark on a celebration of all things gingerbread. As I walked along, I discovered that none of the entries were what I thought of as a typical gingerbread house. Nor were they anything I could ever have made They were amazing, professional creations, clean lines, each a complete vision set forth with edible materials.

Station One belonged to a middle-aged White male chef who'd brought one of his assistants. They were creating a gingerbread scene based on The Nightmare Before Christmas—not my first guess for a holiday-themed creation. It boasted a graveyard, all the major characters from the film, tempting-looking gravestones, and a mausoleum in the background.

The second station, helmed by a Black couple in their 50s, was the Cathedral of Notre Dame. Seriously, the whole thing. The woman was the lead builder. They'd chosen to create it as it was immediately after the fire. It was at least two feet tall.

"Moms of Mayhem" were at the next table. They were very energetic White women who'd discovered a shared interest in food sculpting as they chatted waiting for their young children at the bus stop. They were nearly done with a 1950s-style diner. Not just any diner—it was two stories tall, had a black-and-white tiled floor, and a soda fountain with stools. Vintage convertibles outside were parked by radios made for ordering. Geez.

Emelia and Marta's pirate-themed design was next. A ship sat in the background flying the Jolly Roger. The main sail was fabric, and the small fan sat nearby to blow wind into it during the presentation—her two non-edible items. The pirate chest, however, was the pièce de résistance. It sat in the foreground, on edible sand, open slightly, filled with pearls and doubloons. The colors were eye-catching. I thought they had a real chance at winning.

Gretl Haus' was next. Perhaps not surprisingly, she'd done the witch's house from Hansel and Gretl, an edible mansion with the lines of a cottage (more a mansion) you'd find in the Black Forest.

Hansel and Gretl stood together outside, and the witch could be seen through the door.

The final entry, by a married male couple, was a sophisticated blue and silver landscape, shining with sugar, reindeers, a gazebo and skating pond, and realistic ice skaters in blue and white outfits. Their smiles and seeming forward motion made me fantasize about joining them.

I was glad I wasn't a judge. They were all captivating.

"Contestants, you have an hour. If you finish before that time, please go and dress in whatever you want to wear to present your masterpieces to the judges. You should all be very proud! The hour starts in ten minutes, so finish up and let's wrap this sucker!"

A great thing about the ballrooms was the absence of windows. Under Mom's steady leadership, it was almost possible to forget we were in a white-out blizzard, locked into a hotel with a professional assassin.

Almost.

Marta joined me as I chose one of the remaining sandwiches. I wasn't exactly making do with a leftover, as everything left was appetizing and surprising. I didn't know if Chef Angelica was back running the kitchen, or if she'd decided that since this was Stormie's doing, Stormie would need to feed the troops.

"I'm so nervous!" Marta said. "Emelia really deserves to win! She's worked so hard!"

"She has a good chance," I encouraged. "Even if she doesn't—and they're all so different, who can tell?—she will have acquitted herself very well on national television. Especially for someone so young!"

Marta lowered her voice. "Her family really needs the money. They have lots of medical debt."

"How much does the winner get?" American competition shows always have cash awards. The British seem content to win a cake plate.

"Not much. $10,000. But it's better than nothing. I only wish her great-grandfather could be here!"

"He'll be able to watch it. I have to believe he'll be very proud. At least there's that. And you've done a professional grade job of assisting Emelia."

"Thanks." Marta nodded, then hurried back to her station to the finishing touches onto the pirate ship.

I was getting restless, so I ducked out to see what was happening in the lobby. I even went back to suite seven for a few minutes. I was relieved to find there was still a security person in our hallway, and that he hadn't been shot.

So far, so good.

The room had been straightened, the sofa bed put away, the room service cart removed.

The curtains to the terrace were open. For that moment, it felt as if we were in an AI-generated movie, where no one had bothered to create outside graphics. The world was a freezing white blank slate. I shuddered and closed the drapes.

Then I stretched out on the sofa.

And fell asleep.

I awoke discomfited and unsure. The only rational thought in my head was that I needed coffee. And the quickest place to get it would likely be the crafts table.

The makeshift television studio remained a hive of activity. All the on-air personages were dressed up, their hair and make-up having been completed by Clementine Patterson. Now camera ready, they nervously joshed with each other. Marta must have brought an outfit from home before the storm hit. She'd chosen well. She wore a scoop-neck sweater with a shirt underneath and a pair of black pants. Clementine had cut bangs for Marta and given them a gentle curl. What? Would wonders never cease?

Everyone was called into a circle around the director and the presenter, discussing how the final judging would go. The judges stood at an impartial distance.

I grabbed coffee and took a quick walk along the now-completed gingerbread creations. To amuse myself, I attempted to pick out the two non-edible items in each. It wasn't easy. Everything seemed realistic.

Then I reached the pirate ship. It was easy to spot the sail and fan. I was ready to move on when I saw a new addition: an old-fashioned metal key that had been used to open the treasure chest, now laying on the ground in front of it.

Wow! The key looked real. With a furtive look over my shoulder, I touched it. Then I picked it up.

It was metal. It was a real key. Granted, it went perfectly with the presentation, but it was a third non-edible item. Emelia's project would be disqualified.

I took a breath, and unobtrusively deposited it into my pocket.

The group of contestants broke, with Darla the presenter heading to be miked and the others heading to their places.

Filming lights blasted on. I stepped away, back into the shadows.

Why did I intervene? Had I screwed up? Did Emelia have special permission to add a third object? They were ready to present their works of art to the judges. I couldn't take it back without causing a scene.

Not knowing what to do, I decided to get out before the judging began.

I went to the hall door where the production coordinator glared at me from under her neon-red hair. Perhaps I didn't need coffee, I needed bourbon. I opened the door a foot and slid sideways into the hall.

And smack into the surprisingly barreled chest of Leonard Ruskin.

FINAL HOURS

Ingredients

2 oz bourbon
½ oz gingerbread syrup
½ oz molasses
½ oz heavy cream
1 whole pasteurized egg
Gingerbread cookies
Ice
Cocktail shaker
Cocktail strainer
2 small plates
Coupe glass

Method

Beforehand, chill the coupe glass in the freezer.
Pour molasses onto a small plate. Crush the gingerbread
cookies and put them onto a second plate. Rim the
chilled coupe glass by dipping first into molasses and then
into crushed gingerbread cookies.
In cocktail shaker add, ice, bourbon, cracked egg, heavy
cream, a little molasses, and
gingerbread syrup. Shake ingredients until combined and
a frothy texture is formed.
Strain into chilled rimmed coupe glass.

21

MIDST OF THE STORM

"Mr. Ruskin!" I said. "I was just slipping out before they started shooting again."

"Ah," he said. "We were just angling for a peek inside."

"Oh. Good luck with that."

Leonard Ruskin was now wearing khakis, a pressed blue shirt, and a camel-colored jacket. It fell somewhere in between his Michael Michel look and his "wanna buy a Cézanne?" get-up.

A young teenager stood by him. Ruskin opened the door and pointed something out to the lanky boy, but quickly, before the production coordinator pulled the door shut with a quiet but forceful "Closed set!"

"Apologies," he said.

Both he and the kid backed away and parted company, but not before Ruskin gave the kid a folded twenty-dollar bill.

I wondered briefly what kind of service you could hire a modern teen to do for a lousy twenty bucks and landed on deliver an anonymous note.

I had no intention of waiting around to find out. Ruskin disappeared before I could decide whether the authorities were ready to arrest him or question him or not.

I was staying out of this. Remember?

Much to my surprise, a text dinged on my phone. How did that happen? The cell towers were all down. Maybe a text took such a small amount of energy it could squeeze through? Or maybe it had come through earlier but my phone had only just now roused enough power to notify me?

It was from Noah, the high schooler who lived near the glen in which my cottage nestled.

Mrs. Nash I'm sorry I can't get to your house to feed the dog. Maybe not for a couple days. It's bad out here.

Well, shit. Firstly that he called me Mrs. Nash. There was no one I knew of that name since Mormor died. But mostly because Whistle was now stuck by herself. I didn't know how much food and water Philip had left her, believing Noah would be on it. I didn't care that she would have to relieve herself inside. It could be cleaned up. What worried me more was how cold it was going to get inside the house without heat—especially if no one would be there for days.

Of everything that had gone down the last couple days, the thought of little Whistle freezing to death during this below-freezing storm was the thing that made me nauseous. This one was on me.

Mom found me in the Battened Hatch later that afternoon.

"The shoot is over, Kiddo," she said. "I'm all yours."

"Who won?"

"Winter Wonderland. The shimmery blue and white skating piece."

"Oh. Marta will be disappointed."

"The pirate treasure came in third. Everyone did such a great job. And, given the circumstances, there are no retakes. I am done, done, done." She gave a giant sigh. "The Delicious Network seems good with the content. The entries will look great here in the lobby." She stretched her arms out behind her. Then she noticed. "What's wrong, Avalon?"

"My dog might freeze to death. She's at home in the dark and the cold and I have no way to get to her." And some man was killed on the banquette settee and Philip is out of the country and he'll feel so guilty if Whistle dies and my best friend, who I need more than I thought, is having a crisis of faith at her brother's funeral down in Atlanta—although at least it's a blessing Mom couldn't meet Hannah because I needed one person who was still just mine.

And Marta has bangs.

And the world just carries on being all confused and people are hurting and being mean to each other. People believe lies and hate each other and let the Earth just rot. That's the beginning of my list.

I could have said that to Mom. But she probably would have said something wise and meaningful and then I'd be all mad.

"Hey. They're serving afternoon tea in Pepper's. Let's go sit for a while and figure this out."

Lights were on in the lobby and lilting music played. People were talking and laughing and exiting Pepper's with little carry-out boxes of scones.

When did this happen? Who decided we could be happy in the midst of the storm?

We went and had afternoon tea at Pepper's. There was music on there, too. They were mostly piping in string quartets. People kept coming up to Mom and telling her how much they loved her movies and how funny her Netflix special was and was it fun to work with Ryan Gosling? (Or fill in the blank. They asked about ninety different people she'd worked with.) But they seemed thrilled to meet her and take a selfie with her or get her to autograph their napkin.

Remember that blizzard in Tranquility, Roger? They'd ask in future years. *When Anna Nash was having tea? I have that napkin around here somewhere…*

But the truth is, as much as I fought it, hot tea and scones and light and music and happy people did improve my mood.

I was shocked when Chef Angelica, having discharged her judging duties, came out to chat with folks at the tables. Apparently, tea was her idea.

Wonders were not ceasing, right and left.

"Okay," Mom finally said, "Let's figure this out. There must be a way someone can get to Whistle, even if we can't."

I showed her the text from Noah. "He lives next door."

"Oh. Well. Still. My granddog *will* survive this storm."

"If I can get to the house, even if there's no electricity, we have a fireplace that throws a lot of heat. It can get us through a day or so. But the lodge next door has a generator. If we can make it over there, we'll be fine until the power comes on, even if it's a couple of days."

She looked thoughtful. We both glanced outside. It might not be a total whiteout, but you still couldn't see the lake, separated from us by a sloping hill to the hotel's docks.

Chef Angelica tried to tell Mom the tea was on the house, but Mom insisted on paying and leaving cash tips. Of course.

"Come on," she said, and I followed her out of the restaurant and through the lobby to the registration desk. She waited patiently in line behind a gentleman who was asking if they would be charged for staying extra days, since they would leave if they could.

Two registration clerks were riding out the storm. The one we now waited for was closest to the revolving door. My eyes wandered to the hallway between us and the door, through which the assassin had vanished. From that vantage, I had a clear view of the restroom doors, even if the security camera did not.

I did my best to recall the incident on the footage. The van full of gingerbread shoot people arrived from New York City as the assailant passed by. That person, unnoticed at the time, could have disappeared into one of the restrooms, changed quickly, and blended into the group waiting to check in.

I wanted to see that footage, to see which of the people I now recognized had checked in at that time. And had that person arrived on the van?

Was I reaching? Why would a hired hit person act like they were part of a television shoot, instead of staying out of sight in their room? Unless, of course, they knew they'd need to stay at the inn for several days and would need to blend in and be able to keep an eye on what was happening in the lobby, with the police as well as whatever else was going on.

The snowbound man in front of us moved on and Mom took her place at the registration desk. "Yes, Ms. Leonowens? How can I be of help?"

Leonowens, really? *Anna and the King of Siam?*

"Hi, Charles. If Avalon and I need to get about a mile down the road, in a matter of life and death, what would you suggest?"

Charles looked completely flummoxed. "Ma'am, no one is going out in this storm. There's no way. It isn't safe. Power is out and the roads are closed."

"That's the thing. There has to be a way."

"Did you try asking the concierge?"

Mom and I turned. The concierge desk stood empty.

A cold wind breezed through the revolving door. A pair of adults with two young children stumbled into the lobby. They wore winter coats and boots that were covered in snow. The little girl looked up at me from under her white hood with pink trim. Tears brimmed her eyes. Her lashes were still coated with flakes.

"We made it! Lily! Johnny! We're here! We're safe!" It was the mother behind them. She fell to her knees and brought them into an embrace. The father stood behind them looking snow-shocked.

The door spun again and a figure covered head to toe in winter gear stomped in behind them. Only his eyes were visible. He was tall, over six feet, though his boots had thick soles that might have helped. He looked like the abominable snowman. Then the clue that gave away his identity: the six Siberian huskies outside. It was Roger Woodley, a local jack-of-all-trades. One of his trades was mushing. The dogs, excited and energized, were hitched to a sled. If Lake Serenity freezes in the winter, he gives rides to paying customers. Now, however, he was fetching locals in need who had no heat and no way of generating any.

"This is my last excursion, Charles," he said. "The Kirby family is last on my list. And it's getting so bad out there, I'm taking the dogs back to the kennels. I don't want to get lost on the roads. You can't see two feet in front of your face."

"Thanks," said Charles, as Mr. Kirby stepped up to registration. I knew Glenn would provide them rooms free of charge.

"Where are the kennels?"

This from Anna Nash, looking at Roger with her down-to-Earth, you-might-be-the-only-one-who-can-help smile.

"Two miles on down. I should get started."

"When you say 'on down,' are you heading toward—" Mom looked at me. "What's your street?"

"Cherry Lane."

"Well, yeah, I'm heading straight down Main Street. But it's really bad out there. Not a day for joy-sledding. You can see they're a bit worse for the wear." He referenced the Kirby family.

"We have no interest in joyriding. But if you're passing Cherry Lane, please. Little Whistle is alone and might freeze to death."

"Whistle? Philip's dog?"

Everyone in Tranquility knew Whistle.

Mom took this as a yes. "We're suiting up. We'll be back within five minutes. Please. I've never said this before in my life, but we'll make it worth your while."

He was discomfited. "Five minutes."

Anna Nash and I turned and ran.

MIDST OF THE STORM

Ingredients

> 1 cup green tea
> 1 oz limoncello
> Juice of 1 orange
> 1 teaspoon olive oil
> Ice
> Fresh sliced orange for garnish
> Cocktail shaker
> Collins glass

Method

Tea

> Brew and steep 1 cup of strong green tea. Let cool to
> room temperature, then chill in the refrigerator
> *Cocktail*
> In cocktail shaker, combine ice, chilled green tea,
> limoncello, orange juice, and olive oil. Shake vigorously
> for about 20 seconds to let olive oil emulsify with the
> other ingredients. Then strain into cocktail shaker and
> add more ice to the top. Finish with fresh sliced orange
> for garnish.

22

REALLY DOING THIS

WE RUSHED THROUGH the hallway to suite seven, past the guard, who was watching videos on his phone.

Once inside, I said, "Are we really doing this?"

She said, "Can you think of another way?"

There was no other way.

She went to the closet in the living room where her outdoor coat and boots were stored.

"We might be stuck there overnight. I'm carrying my black bag if you want to stash anything in it," I offered.

"Thanks. I'll grab a couple things. So everyone in town knows Whistle?"

"Everyone in town knows Philip."

"He is quite a guy, Avalon. I'm not only referring to his artistic ability, which is massive. But I asked him, a complete unknown person, to help with the shoot and interact with the contestants, and he pulled it off."

"He wasn't a complete unknown. You said yourself you saw him calming everyone down."

"True."

I found my outwear—winter coat, scarf and one boot, all of which I pulled on. Then I went over to the pile of my dirty clothes from the night before. I dug out the three socks and sat down to put them over the foot that had the cast.

"That won't keep you dry for five seconds," said Mom.

"Could you check and see if housekeeping replaced the laundry bag?"

163

She came out of the restroom triumphantly waving the plastic bag. She sat down in front of me and pulled it on over the socks and the cast.

"All I'm saying is, Philip seems like a good one."

"Yeah, whatever."

"Whatever? Does that mean you're not serious?"

"Mom, we've got to run. Roger looked like he wasn't going to wait for us very long."

"You're right, let's go." She had two pairs of gloves. She handed me one.

"Why would you even ask me that?" I blurted in the hall, to the surprise of security. "You know our family. We don't get serious. We don't stay together. It's fun while it's fun."

"What are you talking about?"

We exited the hall into the lobby. Roger was fidgeting, ready to go. We waved at him and made a beeline.

He nodded.

"I mean, neither of us is exactly married or looking to get married," I gasped as I peg-legged across the cavernous space.

We pulled up sharp in front of our ride. His eyes broadcast his dubiousness about taking us out into the blizzard. "You can't go out in that," Roger said, referencing my laundry-bag wrapped cast.

"I can to save Whistle," I said. "I take full responsibility for getting on that sled."

"We both take full responsibility," said Mom. "We've noted your hesitation."

"Okay, listen. When we go out, we will quickly load you onto the sled. There are blankets, I won't lie, they're pretty wet and heavy at this point. Get under them anyway. Keep your heads down, your hands and feet under the covers. I'm driving, don't forget that. And, whatever you do, don't say anything to the dogs."

"Aye, aye, Capt'n." This was Mom. Roger relaxed a little. Being deemed the captain fit well.

Behind us, Mr. Kirby turned around from registration holding aloft a room key. By now, the kids had moved past their trauma and were skidding around the lobby with wild grins on their faces. When their mother summoned them, they came over directly.

"Are we really staying here?" the little girl asked.

"Yes! We're going to our room and then we can get some food."

Four happy people moved into the hall that led from the other end of the front desk.

Roger gave us a last once-over before plowing back through the revolving door.

"I don't know what you're talking about. Kali and I have been together for twelve years."

"But you're not married, are you? You can break up any time."

She went first through the revolving door, I followed.

We were deposited in another world, one of whipping wind that roared and drove snow by the bucketfuls through the air.

It took hitting the air, the cold, clean air, for my body to realize we were no longer prisoners in a foreboding inn with a murderer. Mom and I were out. We were leaving the once and future danger behind. Yes, we might get into a drifted bank and die upsot, as the song Jingle Bells warned, but it would be a natural death. Of sorts.

To my surprise, two men I knew who worked outdoors at Mac-Tavish's were with the dogs, keeping them calm and the gangline straight. Once we exited the inn, Roger was not playing around. He got Mom situated first, then me behind her. He shoved my cast up onto the sled and tucked the blankets under it. Even if he hadn't told us to keep our heads down and hands and legs under the soggy covers and off the ground, we would have done so out of pure self-preservation.

Behind us in the snow, Roger climbed the runners and put his foot on the brake, ready to release it.

The next things happened simultaneously:

Roger crying, "Let's go!"

Three very loud, very close retorts from a firearm.

My body being shoved forward as someone threw himself onto the sled behind me as it took off at breakneck speed.

And the world was nothing but white.

REALLY DOING THIS

Ingredients

 2 oz whisky or rye
 6 oz apple cider
 1 oz maple syrup
 1 cinnamon stick
 2-3 whole cloves
 1-2 dash Angostura bitter
 Fresh orange peel (for garnish)
 Clear cocktail mug

Method

 On stove top, in medium saucepan on low heat add apple
 cider for about 10 minutes
 stirring occasionally until warm, but not boiling. Add
 clove and cinnamon stick to mixture
 and let infuse for about 5 minutes.
 Mix in whiskey and maple syrup and stir for 2 minutes.
 Remove from heat and ladle into clear cocktail mug.
 Remove cinnamon from pot and
 add into cup for garnish.
 Squeeze fresh orange peel over the top and rim the glass
 for taste and essence.
 To finish, add 1-2 dashes of bitters.

23

THROWN OFF

WHAT?

The gunshots sent the dogs leaping into hyperspace, running so fast it seemed we were preparing to liftoff into the air.

"Gee!" Roger called, and his team obediently turned right and exited MacTavish's. "Haw!" and we made the left onto Main Street.

I sat, nerves taut, Mom in front of me and an unknown person behind me.

Who was he? Did he have a gun? Had we been kidnapped?

I knew we were on Main Street, since I knew the route from exiting the inn. After that, we could have been in Alaska, the Andes Mountains, or Antarctica. There was nothing but movement and blinding snow and a heavy man behind me who may or may not be ready to shoot me.

"Whoa!" commanded Roger. "Whoa!"

Even though I felt the brakes grinding, it took the length of several stores for the team to slow down to the point that we could hear Roger yelling above the driving wind.

"Get off my sled, you sonofabitch!" he said. "Now!"

"Someone is chasing me with a gun!" came the reply.

"Get away from my dogs!"

"I will. I will. Are we near the Michael Michel Gallery? Let me off there. I have a key."

"Easy!" called Roger, and the dogs slowed down.

"You get off when I say we're there."

"Leonard?" yelled Mom. "Leonard Ruskin?"

"Yes," came the reply.

"Someone was shooting at you?"

"Didn't you hear it?"

"Everybody did!"

"You know this guy?" yelled Roger.

"Kind of," yelled Mom

But did we really?

We continued for another minute. The sled was super-gliding.

"Whoa," commanded Roger again. "Whoa!"

This time we did come to a complete stop.

"There's the gallery," Roger said. "Get off."

Tranquility's power was still off. Streetlamps were mostly dead, their solar-powered lights flickering now and then, which was sadder than nothing at all.

Ruskin struggled to roll off the sled behind me.

"Shit," said the musher. "Shit." Then, "Medical emergency. Hiram Foster is having a heart attack. I have to get him and bring him to a main drag so an emergency vehicle can pick him up." There was a brief pause. "I'm sorry, ladies, but I need you off. If you can wait in the gallery with this guy, I'll come back for you as soon as possible."

"What?"

"I'm sorry! Off! It's a matter of life and death!" He was staring at his professional-grade two-way radio.

"Leonard!" yelled Mom, "do you swear you don't have a gun? Do you swear you won't hurt us?"

"I swear, Anna, I swear."

"Please get off, I can't keep the dogs stopped for long," Roger commanded in the same tone he talked to the dogs. It was effective. "I'm sorry, I warned you this might not work."

Leonard Ruskin held out a hand, which I took and clambered off. It was easier for Mom, as she wasn't wearing a cast.

We stood, somewhat shocked, on the sidewalk. Leonard, trying to get his land-legs back, put his head down and walked hard against the snow toward the door of the dark gallery.

Mom and I exchanged looks. What other choice did we have? The sled and the dogs were long gone. We could either follow Leonard inside or freeze to death. While neither sounded appealing, we chose getting out of the snowy blast. We crowded behind Leonard as he fidgeted with a key with shaking fingers. An old-fashioned bell tinkled as he pushed the door open.

The alarm panel was not lit up. Apparently, there was no battery back-up.

I'd never been inside the Welcome Home Gallery when it had no golden glow. It had no glow at all. It was pitch dark, except for a few wall plugs that were programmed to come on when power went off. We stood as our eyes adjusted to the darkness.

Not only was there no light, there was no heat. Still, compared to outside, it qualified as a refuge.

"Leonard, what's going on?" asked Mom.

"Someone is after me. Someone professional. He's going to kill me."

Ruskin was still in his khakis and camel-colored jacket, no outer coat. A man who'd fled into the storm. He not only didn't pull a gun on us, he paid almost no attention to us at all.

"Whoever he is, he's coming. Still coming. I know it. If you're going to be here, you have to hide with me. I have no doubt that once you've seen him, can identify him, he'll kill you too."

I had little doubt of that, myself.

Leonard didn't stop for a minute. He stumbled through the dark to the back hallway, us following close behind. I knew where he was going, of course. I dreaded doing the steps. But there was no choice.

Would the assassin truly follow us here? If there wasn't a blizzard, I'd say a hearty yes—where's the first place you'd expect Leonard to hide? But being an assassin doesn't give you superpowers, and we'd taken the only dogsled in town. How would he get here?

Still, I wouldn't stake my life on the fact he couldn't.

Leonard was in a hurry to get down into the basement. I didn't blame him. It got warmer, more comfortable as we descended. The walls made of huge rock kept the room the same temperature year-round.

He fumbled for the railing in the dark. Mom stopped behind me, turned on her phone's flashlight, and threw the bolt to lock the door behind us. This door also had a non-functioning alarm.

Then she shown the light on the steps as we descended. As we got to the landing, she took my arm and pointed down.

Fresh blood pooled there, a trail behind us and on the steps ahead.

"Mr. Ruskin," she said, "have you been shot?"

THROWN OFF

Ingredients

    2 oz coconut rum
    1 oz Rum Chata Coconut Cream
    ½ oz coconut cream such as Coco Lopez
    ½ cup shredded coconut (sweetened coconut flakes)
    4 oz half and half
    Medium fry pan
    Rubber spatula
    2 small plates
    Ice
    Cocktail shaker
    Martini glass

Method

Coconut

Turn stove top burner to low heat. Add sweetened coconut flakes to pan. Using spatula continue stirring coconut flakes until they turn golden brown. Remove from heat and pour onto small plate, set aside to cool down.

Cocktail

Put a small amount of coconut cream on a different small plate and dip chilled martini glass in cream and then dip into toast coconut to rim glass.

In cocktail shaker add ice, coconut rum, Rum Chata, and dollop of coconut cream. Shake all ingredients for about 20 seconds and strain into rimmed cocktail glass.

24

A SHOT IN THE DARK

HE DIDN'T ANSWER. He blundered quickly down the final stairs, swung behind the staircase, and collapsed in a heap behind the long rows of wine bottles in the corner.

Mom and I came over to him.

"Are you shot?" Mom repeated.

"Seems so," he said.

"Why didn't you say anything? You should have told Roger *you're* having a medical emergency!"

He shook his head. "Do you know how easy it would be for him to find and shoot me in the emergency room? It's the last place I'd go."

"So you'd rather die here." Mom was incredulous.

He closed his eyes. "I would. I don't want to spend my last hours in the hospital in terror, waiting for an assassin to show up. There's a certain adrenaline horror to someone looking you in the eyes and executing you. I'd rather bleed out among art and fine wine."

I might not agree with him, but he did have a point.

"Let me see. Where?"

Ruskin opened his jacket and pointed to his chest, below and to the left of his heart. I wasn't sure what was there. His lungs? Liver?

"Avalon, try to find something to staunch the blood flow," said Mom.

I turned on my cellphone flashlight and looked around. There was a desk which was seemingly used to log the wines, judging from the open ledger before me. I combed through the drawers, pulling out twine and pieces of rope. No help. I found some packing tape, then went over to Michael's paintings. A small piece of thick cloth topped several of them, keeping them from fully leaning against each other. I pulled off one piece.

Mom was bent over Leonard, feeling around his back, between his shirt and jacket. "No exit wound," she said. "The bullet didn't pass through. He's actually not bleeding much, externally. Internally..." she grimaced.

She took the cloth I offered and held it against his shirt. "Why is there a hit man after you?" she asked.

He didn't speak. I was afraid he was going to die right here, in front of us.

Finally, he opened one eye. "I have friends who owned a Newfoundland, a very large black dog. As big as a horse," he said. "The dog was dying and my friend was determined to stay with him till the end. Finally, she had to leave. It's what he'd been waiting for. When she did, he climbed up onto the sofa he wasn't allowed on and died with a smile on his face."

We sat pondering these words.

"I think we should open the Sine Qua Non A Shot in the Dark 2006."

"It's a wine?" Anna asked.

"A fine Syrah. Velvety with intense, layered flavors. Blackberry. Only 442 cases were produced. Not only expensive but *so* good."

"Will Michael Michel be angry?" I asked.

"Hell, yes," said Ruskin. "I'm jumping on the couch."

I certainly wasn't going to miss tasting this.

He told Mom where to find the wine, the corkscrew, and three wine glasses. She gave up holding the makeshift bandage, which wasn't stopping much blood, anyway.

As Anna gathered the items, her flashlight fell on the painted tromp l'oeil walls, town scenes with families playing, shopping, picnicking, done in the more carefree early 1900s. "What is this place?" she asked.

"It's where Michael Michel stores his paintings. And also his wine. Someone painted the walls a hundred years ago or so," I filled her in. "Thanks to the natural climate control of being built into rock in the side of a mountain, things remain well-preserved down here."

"May it be true for us as well," she said.

Mom brought a bottle over to Ruskin, shining the light onto the label. He perused the bottle, a small smile sneaking across his face, and nodded. Mom opened the bottle and brought it over to me as if she was a wine steward. The label was black and white and featured an old-time noir revolver, probably a Smith and Wesson. Seriously.

Mom poured three glasses and distributed them. "We should probably let it breathe," she said.

The art expert scoffed. "Only one of us has time to breathe," he said. "I'm choosing me over the wine."

He inhaled the aroma, delighting in the bouquet. Then he sipped the wine.

"Yes," he said. "This is the way to go."

Mom and I leaned back, sniffed and sipped. I was sometimes afraid I wouldn't be able to tell an expensive wine from a good table wine—but this time I could. I took a second sip and closed my eyes, as Leonard had. Very smooth. I can't tell you I would have said "blackberry" if he hadn't filled me in.

"So," said Mom, "My daughter and I both appreciate a fine wine and a singular story. We have the wine. From what I've gathered, you have a singular story. You don't have to pretend you aren't the mastermind of an impressive art theft operation. We know that, too."

"You talked to Professor Eckhardt?"

"Yes. Well, and local authorities. Wait—you didn't shoot Jules Eckhardt, did you?"

"I don't...shoot people. I'm an art expert."

"We want to believe you," said Mom. "It seems the time to tell your story, if ever there was one."

"First you have to know, I have a great respect for art. And artists. And collectors."

"That's obvious," said Mom. "And yet, you run an art theft ring. Leonard, you've got nothing to lose. As long as you're on the sofa, so to speak…"

It wasn't easy for him to talk. I wasn't sure we'd get a lot out of him.

"It's mostly insurance," he said. "There are two companies who work with us."

"The insurance companies work with you? You're not defrauding them?"

"Art sales and collecting is not supported the way it should be," he said. "Say a museum is struggling financially, might even have to close. But it's deemed unethical for them to sell an important painting to an individual collector. Also, they don't want to advertise their predicament and lose the patrons they do have. If a painting by a famous artist is stolen, or goes missing, they get millions in insurance money. It solves many problems. Later, the person who finds the painting 'on a bus,' as we say, gets five percent of the worth of the painting for turning it in. The insurance company then owns it since they've paid the museum. They are free to auction it or sell it at private sale, pocketing a good chunk of change. Also, the specialized company who handles the sale gets a larger than expected commission."

He took another sip of the Syrah and closed his eyes. "Win, win, win, win." He looked straight at Mom. "Nobody gets shot."

"How do they get the paintings from the museums? Do you have a thief on staff who knows how to avoid all those laser alarms?"

He and Mom were having a good chat. I reclined against the wall.

"Looks good in movies. But no. Eighty-four percent of the staff in art museums have master's degrees yet make less than a living wage. Things can disappear from storage without the drama."

"And the red book you showed me. The paintings whose lines of ownership weren't clean. You obtained those from thieves?"

"Mostly no. Mostly, they're paintings left in wills to deceased persons or found hidden in a barn in France to keep it from the Nazis, or paintings owned by victors in war whose previous owners can't be located. Or private citizens who need the cash from insurance, much as museums do. I like to think we're putting them back into someone's legal possession, so the ownership lines become clean. People can again own and enjoy the art." He tried to take a deep breath and failed. "It's all about the art."

"So if it's win/win/win, why is someone trying to kill you?"

"Things that are lucrative, that are a gentleman's game, often don't stay gentlemanly."

"Meaning?"

"Cosa Nostra. Cartels. They all branch out. They all deal in art. We have a well-oiled system. They want in. No, they want to take over."

"You think you were shot in a mob hit?"

"Likely. A warning to the other gentlemen."

"Any thoughts about the hit on the bounty hunter?"

"Art crime investigations have been getting close for a couple of years now. If I was arrested before the Mob could muscle in, all their hard work would be for naught."

"Is Planton Cavalleros in on this with you?" My first question.

He almost laughed, but it hurt too much. "No. He has a good eye, that's all."

"Do most museums know you do this as a side gig?"

"Hell, no. Ninety-nine percent of my work has nothing to do with art theft."

"How long has this system been going on?" Mom again.

"Almost...a hundred years. As long as gentlemen in insurance and art collectors and museum curators belong to the same men's club." He tried to move, to find a more comfortable position. "You see—you have to understand—that payment for art is seldom fair. To the owner, to the artist, to the agent. What I care about, even with stolen art, is getting it back, getting it seen, getting it properly cared for."

Mom stood and offered Leonard a second pour of the wine. He shook his head. That wasn't a good sign. She recorked and reshelved it. Michael Michel could still have a nice glass if he got to it soon enough.

"I don't want to roll on my compatriots. I also don't want to spend the rest of my life in prison, my reputation in tatters. I just... want... out." He closed his eyes. "The art. Here's the thing. There's an old man. An old man who used to live here. His father was a caretaker for a tuberculosis care house in Lake Saranac. One of the women there gave him paintings for safe-keeping. She thought her husband was going to sell them off for a pittance to people who wouldn't appreciate them or know what they had. I guess you know that. She died. The caretaker died. The old man now has lots of debt. I said if he truly had the paintings, I would make sure he was well compensated as a reward for their return."

"Are we talking about the lost paintings owned by Dora Clarkson?" Mom sounded incredulous.

"Think so. Hope so."

"How was he going to get them back to you?"

Leonard was fading. "Through his granddaughter. She came to town to be in the gingerbread contest. She had the key."

It was my turn to sit up straight. "Is that what you gave that kid twenty bucks to get from the set?"

"Once the shooting was over and things were on display we needed to get the key before anyone else found it or figured it out. It's what I was waiting around for, or else I'd have been long gone by now. But when the kid went to get it, it wasn't there. The joke is, it's likely someone simply took it for no reason, without any idea of what they had."

I took a deep breath. "Could it have been the old man's *great*-granddaughter? Was it the pirate ship and the treasure chest?"

He forced his eyes open. "Yes."

"Did Emelia, his great-granddaughter, know what the key was for?" I asked, holding my breath for the answer.

"No. He asked her to incorporate it so he'd be there with her."
I unzipped my parka and reached into the pocket of my pants.
"Is this it?" I asked, holding up the old-fashioned metal key.

A SHOT IN THE DARK

Ingredients

¼ cup of fresh berries (raspberries, strawberries)
4 oz dry red wine
1 oz Chambord or crème de cassis
½ oz fresh lemon juice
½ oz of simple syrup
4 springs of fresh mint
Splash of sparkling water
Large cocktail spoon (for stirring)
Crushed ice
Wine glass

Method

Fill wine glass with crushed ice. Add red wine, berry liqueur of your choice, fresh lemon juice, and simple syrup. Rip 2 mint leaves in half and put in glass. Stir all ingredients together add splash of sparkling water along with the fresh berries and remainder of whole mint leaves.

25

DYING WISH

"WHERE DID YOU get that?" Leonard Ruskin was gasping for breath but was fully coherent.

"I grabbed it off her display right before the judging. You're only allowed to have two non-edible items. The key made three. It would have disqualified her entry."

"My dying wish," he whispered.

"Leonard, did he tell you where the paintings are?" Mom asked.

"Here. Down here. It's why I came. I wanted to die knowing I was at least close to those paintings."

"You mean, down here, as in this basement?"

"Yes."

"Where?" I asked. "Where could they possibly be?"

"He told me yesterday, when I thought I was about to get the key." Leonard looked over at the painted mouse hole. The one with the keyhole.

I scooted over, Mom behind me. She held the phone/flashlight so I could see the wall. I ran my hand across it. The wall was completely smooth, except for a small indentation where the keyhole was painted. I pushed the key in. It didn't go. It stopped short. I tried again.

Nothing.

I looked again at the wall. There was, indeed, some kind of depression. I tugged at it with my finger. Then, studying the key, I flipped it around and looked at the round bow. I laid it flat against the wall and worked it into the small space then pulled it back towards me.

The mouse door popped open. It revealed a larger door behind it, also with a keyhole. The pirate key fit into this one. I turned it carefully.

This door opened revealing a third door behind it, about four feet by three feet. This one had an old iron lock box mounted on the door itself, so no air, not even a keyhole's worth, could enter the next space.

"Go! Go!" croaked Leonard.

I put the key into the lock. This one took more strength to turn. I could hear the inner workings of the lock clicking and pulling. Then, a final click. I pulled the door open.

Before me was a space that looked like a natural cleft in the rock. A patchwork quilt, with batting inside each square, hung covering some items that were leaning against the wall. I looked back at Leonard.

"Don't just stand there," his eyes pleaded.

Mom came up next to me. Together we picked up the quilt and removed it, along with its contents, from the hiding place. Then we pulled off the blanket. Before us were four rectangular objects covered by an early iteration of what looked to be cardboard. I sent Mom back to the desk in the corner. It had both scissors and a box cutter which she brought over.

Carefully, we cut through the outer layer. Inside, the framed painting was wrapped in a white cotton sheet. Underneath the sheet, we found red felt attached to each corner. Whoever packaged these knew what they were about.

Anna Nash and I carried the painting over to Leonard Ruskin. Only then did Mom turn her phone's flashlight fully onto it.

The three of us stared, slack-jawed and stunned, for several moments. "Mary Cassatt," said Mom, referencing one of the early women Impressionists who found women and children worthy subjects for portraiture, not merely decorative objects.

"It is indeed," said Leonard.

The painting was impressionistic, dots of pastel colors coalescing to make a familial scene. In it a mother and child sat outside under a willow tree. The little girl reclined against the mother. The figures seemed alive, their relationship with each other had an immediacy. I didn't recognize the painting—but I guess that was the point. It had gone missing from art history.

Mom and I took that painting back to the wall and gingerly freed the next one from its protective outer layers. Again, we took it to the art expert who was lying, slumped even farther. Mom turned on the beam of light. "Berthe Morisot," she said.

Leonard nodded.

This painting was also from the Impressionist period. It featured a woman sitting at a table by a window, through which a town was visible. She had a pen and was writing in a notebook.

"Oh!" said Leonard. "Oh!"

He sagged further.

Mom and I were becoming practiced at freeing the canvases. Without consulting each other, we kept the outer wrapping pieces intact as we went.

The third painting I found especially breathtaking. It was a Black woman holding the hand of her young son, both of them standing ankle-deep in water, looking out to sea. This one was pre-Impressionist, the colors more intense. Even in our current less-than-stellar illumination, the shading on the woman's skin was extraordinary.

"It's amazing, but I don't recognize the artist," said Mom.

"Elizabeth Nourse," said Leonard through parched lips. "The first recognized American female artist."

As we went for the last stored painting, he made a circular 'hurry up!' motion with his hands.

The last one was obviously newer than the Impressionists—it featured a boy and his father, and the father was wearing denim jeans. The play of light and shadow was exquisite.

"Abigail May Alcott Nieriker," Mom and Leonard announced, almost simultaneously. "She was the youngest sister of Louisa May Alcott," Mom explained to me.

At this point, Leonard waved Mom and me in close. "You must put the paintings back. You must call Stuart McMillan. Only Stuart. He will know how to care for them, how to bring them back into the art world, into the light."

"Tell me truthfully. Is he in your gentleman's art theft league?" Mom asked, point blank.

"Stuart? No! Not at all. I swear to you. He's the person to handle it. You can't let the police get their hands on them. God knows what would happen. Promise me! Promise!"

"If Stuart is on the up-and-up, we can tell Stuart and the newspaper, also?"

"Yes, yes. Stuart will announce the findings, I'm sure."

"How about Emelia's great-grandfather? Will he get the reward?"

"Yes, yes. Stuart knows how to handle these things. In fact, I need to leave him a voice note on your phone. Please send it as soon as we have cell service. The moment."

Mom got ready to hand him her phone.

"Use mine," I said. "The police are already pulling messages from her phone, but not from mine."

First, he gave me Stuart McMillan's phone number off his phone. Then he took mine. I showed him the voice memo app.

He waved frantically towards the paintings. "Put them back! Please! Quickly!" he said. "Keep them hidden until Stuart arrives."

Mom and I went back to carefully replace each artwork in its bindings. We started with the Cassatt. It was tricky to keep the felt in place on the corners. "Here," she said. "You hold them on the top and I'll pull the sheet tight."

I held the felt in place under the cotton. "Is that how you really feel?" she asked quietly. "That no one in our family stays together?"

"Seems that way," I said.

"Hold the sheet on the top while I place the lower felt pieces. Do you want me and Kali to get married? We'd like to. I was afraid you'd think I was somehow being unfaithful to your father."

"How could you be unfaithful to him when he married Rebecca and has a new passel of kids?"

"This is about him, isn't it?" she asked quietly as we pulled the rest of the sheet taut and reached for the cardboard. A glance back showed that Leonard was trying with all his might to concentrate on the voice message he was recording. He paid us no mind.

Unexpectedly, the simple act of her raising the question about my dad took the breath out of me.

To that day, when I thought of my father, I remembered being maybe four years old, snuggled in next to him, in my bed at night, in my pink bedroom, him reading my favorite books to me—over and over. I remember the white bookshelves, and the care he and I would take picking out three or four books for bedtime. I remember him tickling me as I climbed beneath the covers, his deep laugh somehow also light and delighted, like a brook running joyfully over smooth stones. I remember his smile, how unaffected and proud he was, how I was his and he was mine.

And then he wasn't.

We finished binding the cardboard of the Cassatt with rope from the supply desk. We slid the painting into the crevice and turned toward the Nourse.

"What happened?" I asked, although I was afraid if we talked about him, I might lose my breath, and not be able to breathe ever again. I might die here with Leonard. "What did you do?"

"You do recall what you just said. About him marrying someone else and having a passel of kids?"

"Yes, but something must have happened. To make him change. And leave. He changed. A lot. All at once."

Anna Nash, my mom, who never shied away from anything, did not look at me as she spoke. "You remember your grandparents from when you were young, don't you?"

"Of course."

"But you only remember one set of them. Mormor and Morfar. In Brooklyn."

"Yes."

"It's because your father was cut off from his own parents. They wouldn't speak to him."

"Because he was the black sheep?"

She smiled her crooked smile. "Yeah. They were very religiously conservative. His father was a famous preacher. You know that. They thought Christianity was only good for one thing: Hell avoidance. That God is not a god of love, but of vengeance and, frankly, is petty and easily pissed off. That God created billions of people just to send them to Hell because they didn't get their theology right, even if they hadn't heard about it. Never mind what Jesus said about God being love, about living life in love for other people, taking care of the poor and the displaced, forgiving others, loving justice and mercy. Well, the justice part they might have gone with—as they saw it, but the mercy is out the window. It doesn't track."

She pulled the rope tight around the Nourse and had me put my thumb on the knot while she tightened it. "You want to hear the crazy thing? I met your father in seminary."

"You went to seminary? Why?"

"I am a curious person. It was the only place you could talk about God, in depth, for hours at a time, without people looking at you funny. And about the history of religion. I wanted to figure out how humankind got here."

We successfully replaced the Nourse and moved on to the Morisot.

"Your father had the greatest sense of humor. The best laugh. You could hear him from across campus. He dropped out, though. Even though he was his family's black sheep, was 'sowing his wild oats', it was the *wrong* seminary, teaching the *wrong* things, which made the people in his father's organization petrified someone would find out. It just wasn't worth it to him. He was questioning everything. He wasn't even sure he believed in God. Anyway, we went out for coffee and talked and talked and found we really enjoyed each other's company. We were so happy, just to be together. This was new for him, a revelation. Things were supposed to be hard. One day after we'd moved in together, he told me he sometimes worried about the lack of eggshells. He was so used to having to walk on them."

I had no idea Mom went to seminary. My first thought was gratitude that my friend Hannah, rector of the local Episcopal Church, was out of town or else Mom would have loads to talk to *her* about, too

"Did he leave because you discovered you were lesbian?"

"Hell, no. I loved him—well, the 'sowing wild oats', joyful, fun part of him. I loved the daughter he gave me. I fall for people's spirits, their courage, their kindness and spark. Their genitals are a nice add-on. I would have stayed with him, probably would have married him—that version of him, anyway."

"What happened? How did they get to him?"

We bound the Nourse tightly and placed it carefully next to the Cassatt. Then we turned to the Morisot. "He got saved. Apparently, he didn't see his new happiness as a launching pad for living in love and seeking justice, he agreed when his father's people framed it as sin that was sending him straight to Hell. It seemed he got saved from being a loving, happy person to being a strident, theologically angry one. But that's not how he saw it, of course. He was again in the bosom of his family."

"You threw him out?"

"First off, he was sure we—you and I—were going to Hell, also." She tabbed the corners of the Morisot. I held the felt while she pulled the sheet over. Her voice got quieter. "Do you remember when he started beating you? 'Spare the rod and spoil the child.'"

"I, um, he was already seeing Becca. She already had a kid, too, and taught him how to discipline correctly."

"Yes. She was the daughter of another prominent pastor. I think he learned a bunch of that stuff from her. But you do remember?"

"I remember." A shiver ran through me. "But I didn't mind completely. He said it showed I was his daughter. And... it was the only way he still paid attention to me."

"Oh, hell, no," Mom said, loudly enough that we both checked back over at Leonard. "That is not the message I let my daughter get about buying a man's love and attention. That's when I left him. Maybe you could stand him beating you, but I could not."

Leonard had finished his voice memo. He was now lying full on the floor, my phone in his open hand. "Leonard?" Mom asked.

He nodded and gave a tiny wave.

We put our minds to the Alcott and moved quickly. Once it was safely standing in the crevice of the rock next to the others, we closed both doors and the tromp l'oeil mouse hole to hide the stash. I ran my hand along the smooth wall, amazed at how seamlessly the tiny door blended in, and the painting on the wall, hiding the real door with hinges behind it.

We scooted back over to Professor Ruskin. "They're hidden," said Mom.

"Thank you," he spoke, so quietly we could barely track his words. Then he closed his eyes and was gone.

"Is he dead?" I asked.

"I think he's passed out," Mom said.

She put a hand on his forehead. I extracted my phone from his still-warm hand. I made certain he correctly saved his voice memo and shoved the device into my coat pocket. I also dug under my winter coat to return the metal key to my pants pocket.

Then Mom and I bent close to see if Professor Ruskin was still breathing. He was. Barely.

"What do we do?" I asked. "He didn't want to go to the hospital for fear of the killer, but how could the assassin get there in this weather? And if we told the police he needed protection?"

"How do we get him to the hospital? How do we tell anyone we're here?"

"Roger, the dog team guy, said he'd come back if possible. But he was already concerned about his dogs before the medical emergency."

"Maybe one of us should go up and see what's happening with the storm."

"I'll go," I said.

"Very funny," said Mom, nodding at my cast. "You're the obvious choice."

She stood straight. "I'll see if the storm has let up, or if there's any traffic at all on the street."

I nodded and sat against the wall next to the mouse hole.

Mom climbed the stairs, her phone flashlight aimed before her as she ascended. She opened the door up top and left it slightly open so we could call to each other.

I heard her footfalls as she moved away down the hall into the main gallery.

It was darker than midnight in my secret repository of art and wine. My eyes worked to adjust but even when they had, all I could see were hulking shapes.

And then came a noise, a purposeful, human-generated sound from upstairs. I looked up, curious, as the gallery's front door opened, its welcome bell tinkling.

Was Mom opening the front door to check the street? Had the snow died down?

But then. But then. Then the door swung shut with a violent thud, causing the bell to jangle as if frightened. This was followed by the heavy footfalls of purposeful boots.

Was it Michael Michel, perhaps coming to check on his masterpieces, knowing the security system was down? Why would he make such a journey during a whiteout storm?

Who was it? And why wasn't Mom talking to him?

DYING WISH

Ingredients

> 2 oz chamomile-infused gin (instructions below)
> ½ oz yellow Chartreuse
> 1 oz fresh lemon juice
> ½ oz honey simple syrup
> Sparkling wine (prosecco)
> Edible flowers for garnish to float on cocktail (pansies, violets, or fresh lavender)
> Ice
> Cocktail shaker
> Cocktail strainer
> Martini glass (chilled)

Method

Chamomile-infused gin

> Steep 2 chamomile tea bags in an 8-10 oz bottle of gin for 2 hours. Remove the teabags and strain the gin to remove any loose tea leaves.

Honey Simple Syrup

> Use one part honey to one part water. Simmer on low heat for 10 minutes or until honey is dissolved. Remove from heat and let reach room temperature before use.

Cocktail

> In cocktail shaker, combine the chamomile-infused gin, yellow chartreuse, fresh lemon juice, and honey simple

syrup. Add ice and shake vigorously for about 15-20 seconds and strain into martini glass. Top off cocktail with sparkling wine and float edible flowers on top for garnish.

26
TRAIL OF BLOOD

I HARDLY BREATHED.

Whoever was up there did not call out a greeting. They did not walk casually through the gallery, checking to make sure everything was all right. Even more troublingly, Mom remained silent.

The steps were plodding. As if someone was looking around. Starting and stopping, considering where to go. What to do.

Then they came to a halt, as if the person was looking at something. What did they see?

Then, I knew: Leonard's blood. There was a trail.

They started moving again, at a clipped pace, more purposefully this time. From the sound of the steps, I assigned them a masculine pronoun.

The footfalls entered the back hall that led to the basement door.

It was then I heard Mom's voice. "Will Acton! As I live and breathe. What a relief to see you!"

Her lighter footsteps joined his. "What are you doing here?" he growled.

And I knew—the real Will hadn't miraculously shown up. The assassin had.

"I could ask you the same question," she said, with a distinct smile in her tone. "I'm so relieved to see someone. It's freezing in here. Did you see lights on anywhere? Power, anywhere? And, would you mind not shining that in my face?"

"Wait—you're that actress. Anna, somebody."

"Yes. Anna Nash. Nice to meet you."

"So, why are you here?"

"I got dumped off a dog sled. This was the first open door."

"Dog sled? Did you see Leonard Ruskin?"

"Who?"

"The art guy?"

Their voices became more distinct as they came fully into the back hall.

"I don't know. Something odd happened, and I got kicked off so the driver could take care of a medical emergency. I'm hoping I don't freeze."

"So you haven't seen anyone else since you got in here?"

"No, Will, I haven't."

I wondered if I could hide Ruskin. There really wasn't anywhere to drag him that was completely out of sight.

"Did you notice this blood?"

"Blood? What?"

"All up and down this hall."

"Holy shit," said Mom. "You don't think..."

"Yes. Where there's blood, there's usually someone who's bleeding."

Mom snorted. "Sorry. Sorry. Someone who's bleeding. Just the way you said it. You're a funny guy."

They drew closer to the open door above. So he knew Leonard was down here. I tried to think of ways to get him out, but there was nowhere to move him. I needed to move myself.

I slid back around the corner of the first wine rack.

The footfalls stopped outside the door.

Shit, shit, shit.

The adage 'like shooting fish in a barrel' came to mind. Which is what any assassin could easily do in a space this confined, and him with the only gun.

"Looks like he went down here," said Not Will Acton.

"Could he be dangerous?" asked Mom.

"You! *You*," the newcomer said to Mom, accusatorily.

"Me, what?"

"You were in that movie with Ryan Gosling."

"Yes. Two movies with him, actually."

"Is he as nice as he seems?"

"He is. He's funny, too. You would like him."

"Yeah?"

"Do we have to go down there? It's dark," said Anna Nash.

"I've got to see what's up with the art guy."

"Can you just go and come back and tell me?"

"Nope. You first."

The strong beam of a professional-grade flashlight illuminated the room from the top of the stairs. The killer urged Mom on with a small push. The wood on the stairs groaned with each step they took. I snuck a quick look. I made out his form, the coat, the boots, the hat. It all looked black, in shadow, of course. It was hard to tell anything about him. Yet I would have bet money he was short.

I stayed silent, hardly even breathing.

When they reached the landing, the light swung around, fully surrounding the inert form of Leonard Ruskin at the bottom of the stairs.

"Looks like you were right," said Mom.

"Sit," Not Acton commanded her. It sounded like she sat on the stairs where she had stopped, and he sat behind her.

The beam stayed on Ruskin like a spotlight.

"He isn't moving," said Mom.

"Melissa McCarthy. You were in that movie with her."

"Yes. She is very talented. Very smart and funny."

"Is she still with that guy?"

"Her husband, Ben? Last I heard."

"Ah, well. DeNiro."

"Bob DeNiro? What about him?"

"You been in any movies with him?"

"Never had the pleasure."

They sat for a minute.

"Listen," Mom said. "I know you're not Will Acton. For one

thing, you have a gun at my back, and I don't think Acton has that much gumption. I don't know who you are, and I don't really care. I know you're a funny guy, and a professional. I'm an actor because I find people endlessly fascinating. I've never gotten to actually talk to anyone like you before. Can I ask you some questions?"

"Margot Robbie. Is she that gorgeous in real life?"

"Where is the fairness here? I ask one, you ask one."

"A student of the human condition, are you?"

"Yes. Well put. So. What does it feel like to shoot someone? You must be an expert at it. Is there more of a thrill just before you shoot, or as you're doing it?"

"An interesting question, Mrs. Nash. It's awfully exciting that minute you know it's about to happen. Everything is right, all your planning is paying off. You're where you need to be, the target is waiting, it's all about to happen."

"Kind of like the moment before a first kiss," Mom said, matter-of-factly.

His laugh was a bark. "It's been a while, lady, but sure. I guess. So. Margot Robbie."

"There's nothing bad to be said. I personally think she's even more beautiful in person, with no make-up."

I couldn't believe it. Mom was being held at gunpoint by an assassin, and she was charming the pants off him. So to speak.

"Are there rituals, certain rituals you do before or after you kill someone?"

He thought a minute. "I guess you could call them that. I think of them as habits to ensure safety, after. Checking the area. Moving away but watching. Taking a ring if there is one."

"Do most assassins take a prize?"

"I don't know. I'd bet so. But the occupation, it's got lots of new people. People who think of it as a job. Bang, bang. Might as well send a robot. Just another job. The art of death. It's being lost."

"I can see how that would be disappointing."

There was a pause.

"Ruskin?" The shooter's voice changed to his business tone as he yelled at the man on the floor. Gravelly. "No use playing possum. It's over! You're found out. Either you give my associates entrée into your little art scheme and I help you escape, or you don't, and I use your murder as a warning to what will happen to others who aren't helpful. Either way, I win. Only one way, you live."

Of course, there was no response.

"Do you think he's alive?" asked Mom.

"Not really. You got another question?"

There was a pause. Then, "Will you be sorry to kill me?"

He was quiet. "Yeah," he said. "I really will."

My heart revved. My mother comes to visit me and is shot dead for her efforts. In front of me. Though there was no way I wouldn't be dead seconds behind her.

There was only one way out, one staircase, and on it sat a guy who killed without remorse.

"I haven't seen him move since we got here," Mom said, referencing Ruskin.

The attention turned again to the man on the floor. I took that split second to peek around the corner. Thank God, Mom was hoping for such an action. We locked eyes. I made the smallest nod, indicating she needed to get him down here.

No matter what happened, I would have to come at him from the front. I would have approximately one half of one second before he realized there was a third conscious person. One half of a second before he turned his gun on me, and Anna and Avalon Nash were both deceased.

If I had time, I'd be sick.

"Look, why don't we just make sure the art guy is dead, so we can go upstairs?" This was Mom.

"You wanna see me shoot him?"

"No. Not even for research. I truly don't."

"Come down the stairs."

Both of them descended.

"Now you, don't move. If you do, I have to kill you. And who knows? Maybe I won't have to, after all, if you're a good girl."

Good girl? Okay, that guy was as good as dead, if my mother had anything to say about it.

Meanwhile, I had half a second.

Fuck, fuck, fuck.

The killer came down the final steps. He took a step towards Ruskin, aiming his gun.

I ran towards him, coming in from a slight angle. He looked at me, chortled, and was in the process of swinging his gun around when I whacked the side of his head, hard, coming up from below, with a 1993 Leroy Chambertin Grand Cru.

He collapsed to the ground.

"Fuck," said Mom. "Are you okay?'

TRAIL OF BLOOD

Ingredients

3 oz red wine (cabernet or malbec)
1 oz dark rum
1 oz cherry liqueur
¼ cup of whole black peppercorns
½ oz black peppercorn simple syrup
½ oz orange blossom water
Fresh slice of orange for garnish
Cocktail spoon (for stirring)
Sparkling Water
Ice
Collins glass

Method

Black peppercorn simple syrup
In medium saucepan add 1:1 ratio of water to sugar and peppercorns. Put on low heat for about 10-15 minutes, stirring occasionally. Remove from heat and bring to room temperature before straining and discarding peppercorns.

Cocktail

Fill collins glass to top with ice. Add red wine, peppercorn simple syrup, dark rum, and cherry liqueur. Stir all ingredients together and finish with sparkling water and a fresh orange slice.

27

WAITING

"Is he dead?" I asked.

"Not yet. Quick, before he wakes up."

Our teamwork on the paintings made it easier for us to tackle the killer's body together. First, Mom grabbed his gun and shoved it into the middle drawer of the desk in the corner. She then brought the rest of the rope. We rolled the inert assassin fully onto his stomach and pulled his arms behind him. I held his wrists together as she bound them. I was afraid he'd die, more afraid he'd wake up. She tied his legs together, using some impressive knots. Anyone else would ask which movie she'd learned them for. I didn't care.

Next, his feet. Then we used a strong length of rope to tie his hands and feet together.

He groaned but didn't awaken.

"We've got to get help," Mom said. "Let's think. How do we get a signal out when all communications are down?"

Somehow, that wording jogged my memory. I slid over to my bag and withdrew the personal locator beacons Inspector Spaulding had given me. Each box had simple instructions on how to activate them. I stuck one into the assassin's pocket, in case he managed to get away.

"I'm not completely sure this signal can get through the rock down here," I said.

"Take that one upstairs into the main room. Take a look outside, while you're at it."

"I don't want to leave you down here with them."

"I don't want to leave the two of them alone down here."

"Understood. I have this fricking cast. Do you want to go up again?"

"Hoping against hope someone will reply to our bat signal, it would probably be good if you were the first person they saw."

I nodded. I took the other locator and climbed the steps faster than I would have thought possible. The minute I was up, I turned it on.

Suddenly, there was cold and space and air and I could breathe. I put the activated locator on the table next to the back hall entrance and hobbled to the front door. The state of the pried lock left the door handle loose.

I dared open the front door a couple of inches. Snow. Driving snow. Not another living soul. Night was falling. The sky was black behind the storm's darkness. My last flicker of hope blew sideways.

I closed the door and hobbled back to the open basement door. My adrenaline was pumping. "You okay?" I asked. I desperately wanted to do something, but there was nothing else to be done.

"Aye, aye," Mom said.

I sat on the top step. "Do you remember that time in Budapest when we got trapped in that castle?" I asked.

She laughed. "You mean, when that guard had to climb through the battlement on his stomach to pry the door? Wasn't that the best?"

We fell silent again. At one point I heard a groan.

"Gun guy," said Mom.

Five minutes later, a strange sound echoed through the front gallery. A ringing sound. At first I couldn't place it. It wasn't the bell over the doorway. I heaved myself up and went in that direction. And there, sitting on the gallery manager's desk, was a corded landline telephone plugged into a wall phone jack.

I picked up the receiver. "Hello?" I said.

"Nash. What now?" Inspector Spaulding said.

"Oh, God, Mike!" I blurted, then got control of myself. "The mob assassin has been whacked on the head and is out cold, tied in ropes. Leonard Ruskin, the art theft guy, was shot by him and is dying. Can you get somebody here? Except Ruskin and assassin-guy can't go to the same hospital because the assassin would still kill Ruskin."

"Is this a prank?" asked someone with a gruff voice behind him.

Whatever response Mike gave shut him down.

"Who is there with you?"

"And conscious? Only my mother."

"Are you all right?"

"Until the assassin wakes up."

"But he's bound?"

"As well as we could do it."

"Help is on the way," Mike said. "Now. Tell me everything you just told me. Slowly. With details."

"Hang on," I said. "Let me holler down to my mother. I'll be right back."

I was never gladder to leave a corded phone off the hook in my life.

"Mom," I said, "help is on the way. Are you okay down there?"

"Yes," she said. She spoke as quietly as possible to be heard. We didn't want to startle the assassin awake. "Especially knowing some-one's coming."

The cavalry arrived in less than twenty minutes. Even though I was on the phone with Mike the whole time, it still seemed like for-ever.

Given that Tranquility is in the mountains, the state police have interesting vehicles to traverse driving snow. The lead vehicle was a heavy-duty emergency vehicle with ski-type apparatus where the giant wheels would normally be. The vehicles behind it had those enormous wheels.

I had Mom come up so we wouldn't be found and somehow trapped down with the perps while the cops did their thing.

They rushed in, in a group, with heavy snow coats and hats, flashlight beams shattering the darkness. The lead investigator was talking to Mike on his walkie.

"You okay?" he said gruffly to us. We nodded, then pointed to the back hall. They trudged in that direction. A young woman I hadn't seen before stayed with us, checked our identification and told us Inspector Spaulding would talk to us in person in the next couple of days, instructing us not to leave town. We tried not to laugh. The blizzard continued. Merely leaving the gallery looked impossible enough.

If there's one thing I've learned, it's that anything having to do with law enforcement takes a very long time. This incident took less time, probably because the two gentlemen in question needed immediate medical attention. Leonard and Not-Will were removed in separate vehicles.

Mom and I remained upstairs. I was chilled to the bone and worried about Whistle. We'd lost our only way to reach her, or anyone, for that matter. So I was happily surprised when we were offered a ride home on that huge ski-themed mega-truck. Mike probably had something to do with it. "Have you got some source of heat in the house?" asked the officer in charge.

"Yes, I have a gas fireplace with a pilot light. It throws a lot of heat."

Usually, I'm proud to show off the glen in which I live, the large lodge belonging to my landlord, and the fairy tale cottage I claim as mine. Of course, you couldn't see any of those things. To my profound relief, the truck pulled into the hidden dale, past the parking area, past the lodge and right up to the footbridge leading to my place. Two state police officers hopped out with shovels and actually cleared the bridge, the walk, and the stairs to the front door. Their high beams shone like one of those tractor beams used by UFOs in movies. Though I usually entered through the back door, I did have the front door key in my bag.

We went inside. The trooper handed me both a lantern and a kerosene heater and shook our hands before they left. Apparently, catching two crooks and leaving them tidily waiting to be picked up by the authorities comes with some perks.

Inside, Whistle looked at me with happy eyes that said, "I knew you'd come, and here you are!"

I let her out to do her business on the stoop, then she came inside, where I flicked on the fireplace gas and lit the pilot light while Mom set up the portable heater. The lantern threw enough light to make the place seem cozy.

"No one is staying at the large lodge," I said. "If we can make it over there, I believe there is a working generator."

The two of us stood by my large glass front window, staring at the raging snow which revealed nothing behind it.

"I'd prefer not to go out again," said Mom. "Have you got any wine?"

WAITING

Ingredients

2 oz white tequila
1 oz Tequila Rose liqueur
Fresh strawberries
Cocktail shaker
Strawberry rope licorice
Ice
Rocks glass

Method

In cocktail shaker add ice, tequila, and Tequila Rose liqueur. Shake cocktail vigorously and pour into rocks glass. Add a strawberry to side of cocktail glass and cut each end off a piece of strawberry rope licorice to act as a straw.

28

THE MORNING AFTER

I THOUGHT EVERYTHING we'd been through would keep us wide awake long into the night. I was wrong.

We grabbed fruit and wine from the kitchen, and blankets and pillows from the linen closet and bedrooms. Shortly after ten o'clock the adrenaline left our bodies and we crashed.

Whistle, too.

It was light outside when I awoke. A look out the window on the way to the bathroom confirmed the storm had passed. The snowfall outside was at least two feet, with drifts as high as four or five feet. There was still no power.

I took the shovel Philip had left by the back door and cleared a small path for Whistle on the back patio, then gave her breakfast and clean water. The night before, I'd taken two breakfast burritos from the Cardamom Café, my favorite local restaurant, out of the freezer. They were nicely thawed. I poured water into the kettle and lit the burner, readying the French press we kept for just such occasions.

When I went back into the living room, Mom was returning from her bathroom. She sat on the floor against the sofa, pulling her blanket on top of her. She'd brushed her hair and splashed (very cold) water on her face. She wore a white shirt and jeans and the red hoodie I'd loaned her the night before when her sweater felt itchy. She looked young and fresh and normal.

"Morning," she said.

"Morning." I knew she took her coffee black, so I poured her a mug, and handed her the plated burrito. "It's my favorite, from my local breakfast place. Banana coconut curry. I always keep some in the freezer for situations such as this."

She took a bite. "Very tasty," she said. "And I love your place."

I looked around at the chintz fabrics and the flowered pillows. We both knew it wasn't my style. But it was nice, in a throwback kind of way. "The whole place was created by a Hollywood set designer. Philip grew up here—but he says it looked very different then. Very 2000s. After he, his mom, and brother moved out, his gran restored things to the original décor. He says it's a totally different experience living here now."

"Very homey," she said.

"It's funny you should say that. I've been thinking about hiraeth lately—the longing for a true home, one that may or may not actually exist. My heart is broken because my *mormor* died. I wasn't considering that you lost your mor, your mother.

"Not to mention," I continued, quickly, while I had my nerve, "the family's Brooklyn brownstone probably feels like hiraeth to you and your brothers and sisters. It really isn't fair for them to put it on you to keep it intact, or, conversely, to blame you for taking their family home away from them, from all of them. It really isn't fair."

She obviously wasn't expecting this. She put down her burrito.

"I appreciate that you came here to talk to me about it, instead of just announcing the sale. I'm sure it wasn't easy for you."

"I never know," she said.

"What?"

"How to be with you. How to arrive. Let you know, or show up? You're never happy to see me. You've made it clear that simply by coming to a place, I ruin the entire town for you. I steal your friends. I become a shadow-casting legend and you can never be viewed the same. I get the message—stay away or ruin your life."

She picked up the coffee and sipped it. It was still a bit too hot. She put it down.

"What am I supposed to do if the person I love most can't stand to have me around? What do I do? I never went into this profession for the fame. If I could cut off that part, I would, happily. I am not on social media. I don't participate in 'Hollywood' or go to any openings for films I'm not in. But even if I quit acting now, it wouldn't go away."

"Why... why would you want to be around me? When you're with anyone else, you're 'on,' you're charming, you hear every word they speak, you say amazing things they've waited their whole life to hear. And when you're with me, half the time I don't think you're even paying attention." Whoa. But this might be my one chance.

"I only... I feel like I don't have to be 'on' when I'm with you. I'm sorry if it feels like I don't pay attention. Like I don't see you. But you're part of me. You're inside me, not separate, across from me." She stopped. "I can see how that's my take on it and... it might not come off that way."

She started to cry. Quietly. Tears pouring down her cheeks. "It's not just this," she said. "It's everything."

It came clear to me. How, not counting Kali, she was alone in her own family. Especially with Mormor gone now. Granted, her brothers and sisters were significantly older than she was, but it went beyond that. They thought she had everything, needed nothing. They thought they should save their house. The family. Save them all.

And her own daughter wanted nothing to do with her, wanted her nowhere in the vicinity.

It's hard when you realize when your actions have deeply wounded someone. Yet the circumstances that caused your self-protective actions have not changed.

I guess I had to grow up. I just wasn't sure how.

I'd have to be courageous. I'd have to believe in myself enough that I could withstand—not yet embrace, that's for sure—Anna Nash being my mother.

I'd have to be my mother's savage daughter.

I laughed. And, swear to God, at that moment, the power came back on.

THE (SNOWY) MORNING AFTER

Ingredients

2 oz vanilla vodka
2 oz white chocolate liqueur
Dash of almond extract
1 oz half and half
Small amount white chocolate syrup (melted white
chocolate chips)
Edible pearl dust
Martini glass (chilled)
Ice
Cocktail shaker
Cocktail strainer
1 small plate

Method

On small plate add white chocolate syrup and dip martini
glass to rim.
In cocktail shaker add ½ & ½, vanilla vodka, and white
chocolate liqueur, and dash of almond extract. Shake
ingredients vigorously and strain into martini glass.
Sprinkle edible pearl dust on top of cocktail for garnish.

29
THOSE SHIPS DID SAIL

THREE DAYS LATER I was behind the bar in the Battened Hatch, as usual. Happily, I was no longer stuck there because I was wearing a cursed cast. I could walk the room whenever I pleased. When I was finally able to see my orthopedist after he'd set all the storm-related broken limbs, he'd deemed my sodden cast unredeemable and cut it off. He did not feel it needed to be replaced.

Roads were cleared. We were plowed and shoveled the rest of the way out. It was already slightly above freezing, thus the snow on the roads was turning to slush. I hoped it would remain intact in the higher elevations to give the ski areas a boost into the winter season.

Anna Nash, my mother, sat at booth three, her regular booth, talking to Professor Jules Eckhardt, who had been released from the hospital. Mom was planning to use her film production company to make a movie about Jules' life, which Mom would direct and star in. It would culminate with solving the gentlemen's art theft plot.

Leonard Ruskin died on the operating table. Turns out the bullet that hit him as he fled his attacker lodged in his liver. He likely would have died even if he'd gotten to help faster. It turned out his gentleman's art club wasn't quite as gentlemanly as he'd let on, nor was win/win/win quite as prevalent as he'd led us to believe. Also, there was a purple book for those collectors who were less honorable than those shopping from the black and red. This information didn't enhance Leonard's legacy but it did give Mom and Jules a better movie.

I sent Leonard's voice memo, as requested. I kind of understood how Leonard could not see a clear path forward after being caught (he was under arrest before they checked him into the hospital) and he saw dying as his best outcome, but I was sorry he was gone, anyway.

I don't know what happened to the other guy. His name wasn't Will

Acton, it was Frank Cottle and he was a wanted hit man. He disappeared into the murky landscape of apprehended Cosa Nostra felons. Mike told me I was listed in the police report as a 'concerned local citizen'. Mom was called 'citizen number two'. This lessened the chance anyone would come after us.

That morning, Marta stood beside me, sketching ideas for future gingerbread contraptions on a phone app. She was sad Emelia had come in third, as her family needed money very badly. The Delicious Network loved the special and was editing it with lightning speed. Each of the contestants were paid for expenses and a basic daily rate, which, honestly came out to about the same as the top prize. That helped. I didn't want to tell Marta about the rediscovered paintings, not until we knew how everything would shake down—if Emelia's great-grandfather would see any reward, given Leonard's death.

Mom told her siblings she couldn't buy the brownstone. If they all wanted to chip in, if they all wanted to be active participants in its upkeep and running it, she'd reopen the discussion. No one said yes. So she invited everyone for a last minute Thanksgiving dinner in Brooklyn to say goodbye to the place together. Everyone complained because they had plans. Then everyone cancelled their plans and agreed to come, including my favorite cousin Reggie. I agreed to come as well.

It was the whole hiraeth thing. For me it was compounded by Mom and Kali deciding to sell the house I grew up in. I tried to concentrate on the happier consequences of our discussions, Mom's and mine. In practice, I had two moms. Now, maybe Mom could have a spouse as well.

I hoped Philip would be back in time to come to Brooklyn with me for Thanksgiving. So far, there had been no happy ending for him in Paris.

The lunch rush was over. I was creating a new drink menu for Thanksgiving when a tall, patrician White man walked in. He wore a long coat and a navy blue felt fedora. He exuded confidence. He had a thin face, a thin nose, and eyes that took in the whole room. Whatever company he was with, he was the one who ran the meetings.

Once he'd perused his surroundings, he came over to me and put his hat on the bar. "Hello," he said. "I'm looking for Ms. Nash."

I was about to point, with a roll of the eyes that conveyed anyone with half a brain could see she was in booth three.

Till he continued, "Avalon Nash."

"Present," I said.

A slight, satisfied smile crossed his face. He offered his hand and we shook. "Stuart McMillan," he said. "I believe you sent a voice message from my colleague, Leonard Ruskin?"

"I did," I said. "You'll understand why I ask, but may I see some identification? I need to make sure you are who you say you are."

"Good thinking," he said. He took out a driver's license and a faculty ID card.

Once he did, I Googled his name and found many, many photos of him. As I was doing this, he took off his wool coat, folded it, and put it on a bar chair next to his. "So, I'll be needing three things," he said. "The key to the hiding place of some long missing paintings. An introduction to a painter named Philip Young. And a strong drink."

"Two of them will be no problem," I said. "Though I'm sorry to disappoint you, but Mr. Young is in Paris."

"Ah. Is there any way he would give me access to his studio? With an overseer, of course."

"It's unlikely, but I could try to find out. What drink would you like? I recommend one called Paintings at Sunset."

"All right. Meanwhile, point me to the restrooms. I'll be back."

He left. I grabbed my cell.

"Is that Stuart McMillan?" Mom asked, leaning against the bar.

"Yes. How did you know?"

"Googled him immediately after the power came on."

"He wants to see Philip's studio. I'm certain Philip won't want anyone in there until it's all straightened up."

"Are you kidding?" Mom said quietly. "When I was there with Ruskin, it felt cool and special to be in there when we weren't expected. Like we really were in on the ground floor of something before anyone else saw those paintings."

I'd hit the call button on my phone. Philip's number was ringing in Paris. I didn't really expect him to pick up. "Hey, Av," he said.

"Hey. This guy named Stuart McMillan is here—well, now he's in the restroom—but Ruskin told him about you, sent photos I think, and he wants to see your studio. No, right? Is there a time I should tell him to come back?"

"Stuart McMillan?" Philip asked, his voice laced with incredulity. "*The* Stuart McMillan?"

"Yeah."

"Let him in. Tell him it's a mess. Tell him I was painting, then I had to leave town. Tell him not to take photos without asking me. But tell him I'll let him—and only him—in."

"You tell him. Okay?"

Mr. McMillan wound his way back to the bar. I held out my phone. "Philip Young," I said. "He's in Paris."

"Philip Young? Stuart McMillan," he said in a suave, assured voice. He took my phone and headed back into the hallway.

In the background, Professor Eckhardt gathered her papers and headed for the lobby door. She waved at Mom as she passed by. "Talk to you soon," she said.

Anna Nash sat down in front of me in one of the comfortable cushioned bar chairs. The very one in which she'd been sitting five days before. "So this is your life," she said.

"Yup," I said.

And we both smiled.

PAINTINGS AT SUNSET

Ingredients

1 ½ oz white rum
1 oz passion fruit liqueur
½ oz orange liqueusr
½ oz simple syrup
½ oz lime juice
1 small pinch of edible silver glitter
Fresh passion fruit (cut in half leaving seeds inside)
Cocktail shaker
Ice
Rocks glass

Method

Add ice white rum, passion fruit liqueur, orange liqueur, simple syrup, lime juice, and small pinch of edible glitter to cocktail shaker. Shake vigorously for 20 seconds and pour into rocks glass. Add half of passion fruit to the top of drink for garnish.

AUTHOR'S NOTE

ONCE AGAIN, I offer my gratitude to the fine people of Lake Placid, New York, as well as the neighboring community of Saranac Lake. Saranac Lake was indeed well known for treating tuberculosis patients with plentiful fresh air, both in cottages and in a sanitorium, from 1873 to 1945. The town's population began to grow after well-known guests such as Robert Louis Stevenson came to stay (one winter was enough for him, he headed for the south seas) and after the first trains arrived, making the area more accessible. You can still tour the Stevenson Cottage.

"My Mother's Savage Daughter," in the style of a Viking drinking song, is by Karen Kahan, writing and recording as Wyndreth. I recommend purchasing her album on bandcamp: https://wyndreth-savagedaughtershieldmaid.bandcamp.com/album/my-mothers-savage-daughter-original-1997-release

Thanks, as always, to early readers, including Rebecca Cantrell, Barb Sherer, and the artists of the Haven, especially Crystal Paul Watson, Sharrata Hunt, Jean Stevenson and Anne Pell Harkness.

Thanks to my copyeditor Sarah de Souza and inimitable proofreader, Gillian Freed. Thanks, too, to cover creator David Colón.

As always, I offer my undying gratitude to Jamielynn Brydalski, one of the best mixologists on the planet, who created the drink recipes. Avalon is lucky to have such talent behind her.

Cheers!

SHARON LINNÉA
Horseshoe Mountain, North Carolina
July 2024

Sharon Linnéa is the author of the Bartender's Guide to Murder mysteries, including *Death in Tranquility*, *Death by Gravity*, *Death Among the Stars*, and *Death from Beyond*. She also wrote the bestselling Eden Thrillers (*Chasing Eden*, *Beyond Eden*, *Treasure of Eden*, and *Plagues of Eden*) with B.K. Sherer. She has written award-winning biographies of Raoul Wallenberg and Hawaii's Princess Ka'iulani, along with a dozen other titles. She had a memorable time as a TIPS certified bartender. She now lives outside Asheville, North Carolina.

Jamielynn Brydalski is a mixologist who grew up with a passion for the art of food. After studying hospitality at Paul Smith College, she fell in love with the art of crafting specialty cocktails while traveling the world. She has won international awards for her creations. She met Sharon while she was bartending in Lake Placid, New York. The rest is mystery, er, history.